Praise for Beth Williamson's
Devils on Horseback: Nate

"When I am in the mood for an exciting, passion-filled western historical romance, I turn to Beth Williamson. She never fails to capture the emotions of her characters, and her books always grip me from page one and refuse to let go. *Devils on Horseback: Nate* was this type of novel. Beth Williamson's books should never be missed... Nate's story deserves two thumbs up and a huge Rebel yell. Yee-haw!"

~ *Talia Ricci, Joyfully Reviewed*

5 Blue Ribbons "...a phenomenal story. DEVILS ON HORSEBACK: NATE is one of those old-fashioned romances that just warms a reader heart and soul. Beth Williamson has a true gift of creating such real and gritty characters. You have the hero, the damsel in distress, and of course, the villain with a dash of mystery to spice up the mix. Combined with an explosive plot line, an exquisite romance and some very tasty sex, this story will leave you burning for more from this riveting author..."

~ *Amanda Haffery, Romance Junkies*

Devils on Horseback:
Nate

Beth Williamson

A Samhain Publishing, Ltd. publication.

Samhain Publishing, Ltd.
512 Forest Lake Drive
Warner Robins, GA 31093
www.samhainpublishing.com

Devils on Horseback: Nate
Copyright © 2007 by Beth Williamson
Print ISBN: 1-59998-659-0
Digital ISBN: 1-59998-485-7

Editing by Sasha Knight
Cover by Scott Carpenter

First Samhain Publishing, Ltd. electronic publication: September 2007
First Samhain Publishing, Ltd. print publication: November 2007

Dedication

To my wonderful, fabulous, amazing editor, Sasha, a woman who gave me the opportunity to fly on the wings of words. Hugs and smooches.

Prologue

April 1865

Nate couldn't hear over the roaring in his ears. The acrid stench of charred wood wafted toward him and he tried not to breathe too deeply.

Gone.

Everything was gone.

The five men sat atop their horses on the rise overlooking their home town of Briar Creek, still as statues. Nate was certain everyone felt the same kick to the chest. Their town, their homes, their lives. Gone. They'd come so damn far to get back home, had cheated death, even survived a trip into the bowels of hell.

Home was simply gone.

Not only was the Blackwood Plantation house in rubble, but the fields around it completely destroyed, and likely salted. Miles and miles of devastation with decaying carcasses of cows, goats, hell, even looked like the chickens had been slaughtered.

"Jesus Christ." The words burst from his chest like a gunshot.

He spurred his horse into a gallop, ignoring Gideon's shouts. He flew over the ashes and soot, sending clouds of dark death around him. At that moment, he didn't give a shit if it killed him. He had to see what had happened to his own home, especially if the mighty Blackwood home had suffered so greatly.

Leaning over the horse's neck, he urged Bonne Chance on, keeping himself as small as possible on the gelding's back. The warm spring wind whipped past him, a few insects slammed into his face, but he kept going. He knew he looked like a madman, but it just didn't matter. The sound of the hoofbeats echoed through his heart. God, please, let the house still be there.

As he rounded the curve in the trail that led to his father's house, in his heart he knew he'd find nothing. Or worse.

What he didn't expect was to find a mummified body hanging from the magnolia tree he played on as a boy, nor the blackened pit that had been his childhood home.

Nate didn't remember getting off the horse, or falling to his knees. He belatedly realized the howling he heard was coming from his throat. Long, gut-wrenching sobs that wracked him to his core. His stomach roiled and what little food he'd eaten in the last day came back with a vengeance. A wet handkerchief was placed in his trembling fingers and a hand landed on his back.

"Easy there, Lieutenant, easy." Gideon's voice broke through the blackness that surrounded him.

"Is he okay?" Zeke asked.

"Hell no, he's not okay. Can't you see he's puking his guts out?" Lee shot back. "Probably upset he's ruining his fancy britches too."

"Shut up, Lee," Jake interjected. "That's his daddy hanging there. Have a little respect."

A snort was Lee's only response.

Gideon leaned down close and spoke in Nate's ear. "We'll cut him down and bury him proper. You just get your breath back."

His former captain left him on his knees in the dirt and directed the rest of the men to take care of the body.

Nate struggled to his feet. "I'll be all right. I-I can't let you do this for me."

"We'll just help you get the hole dug then." Gideon nodded at the others and they all got to work.

Briar Creek's famous sons had finally come home.

Chapter One

June 1865

Nate Marchand was so hungry he seriously considered cutting up his belt and boiling it to make soup. There had to be at least something left of the cow in it. The only thing stopping him was the fact that without the damn belt, his trousers would be down around his ankles. He refused to face starvation with a bare ass.

So far, D.H. Enterprises had amounted to a load of shit. When Gideon suggested they start their own business, DH Enterprises, it had seemed like a wonderful idea. However, after a month, not one job had come their way. Oh, they worked their asses off, mostly mucking out barns, or digging new holes for outhouses. Jobs that would have been beneath them before the war. Gideon tried to keep everyone positive, but the truth was, they weren't far from begging for food. More than once, they'd had to share a fish or a squirrel they caught between five of them. Some days, there wasn't any food at all.

The five of them had headed west to rebuild their lives, to find what was taken from them, to regain what they'd lost. Pick a reason. It didn't matter exactly why, just that they'd left Georgia to never return. After two weeks, their bellies were as empty as their pockets. They were desperate and they had all turned to Gideon for guidance.

They'd all jumped at the idea of DH Enterprises. DH stood for Devils on Horseback, their nickname during the war. Their business hadn't earned them much except sore backs and short tempers.

Nate didn't like the feeling of not being in control. He was determined to find them work and he vowed to end their losing streak. Now that they'd landed in the small town of Grayton, and had set up camp in a clearing with a stream and some shade from the hot Texas sun, Nate wanted to get right off to town to sniff around. He was itchy and restless to do something.

"Where are you going, Nate?" Gideon asked as he unsaddled his horse.

Nate met his blue gaze. "I'm heading into town to find out if there are any jobs hereabouts. My stomach's about to touch my backbone, Gid."

Lee laughed. "No news, Frenchie. You're already as skinny as a rail."

"Shut up, idiot." Nate headed for the stream to refill his canteen. It never failed. Lee always had a smart remark ready for him. Nate tried to ignore him, but it was hard. What he really wanted to do was pop Lee in the nose, but he didn't want to start a war. He'd had enough of brothers fighting already.

Nate washed his hands and splashed water on his face. After rinsing the dust off, he stood and wiped his wet hands on his pants. He grimaced at the condition of his clothes, but it couldn't be helped. He'd have to rely on his brains and charm, he thought with a wry grin.

He walked back to the camp and took his gelding back to the stream. Bonne Chance was a sorrel that he won in a poker game right before the war. He was an even-tempered horse that had the endurance of a thoroughbred. Nate knew the horse was tired, but hunger came before comfort. After the horse drank his fill, Nate swung up into the saddle and headed toward town.

ഇൗൽ

Grayton was a typical small town, with a few permanent buildings and a lot of wood-front buildings in sore need of repair. He was happy to note a church and a stone jail. That meant the townspeople had money to spend. If they were lucky, they had some to spend on D.H. Enterprises.

Nate headed straight for the building marked General Store. As he dismounted, he nodded and tipped his hat at two older women walking down the wood-planked sidewalk. They nodded back and continued on. Since the townsfolk weren't snubbing him, it was another good sign for DH Enterprises. He could almost taste a ham dinner. With potatoes and greens.

The front door opened, a bell tinkled and a man walked, no, swaggered out. He was in his fifties, with steel-grey hair, a black hat and a suit that was obviously not purchased in this general store. Nate knew instinctively this was a man with deep pockets. He stepped toward the man and held out his hand.

"Good afternoon, sir. Nate Marchand at your service."

The man's blue eyes were nearly colorless and as sharp as the knife resting in Nate's boot. "Afternoon, stranger. What do you want?" He did not offer his name and ignored Nate's proffered hand.

"I noticed you leaving the store and I wondered if I could ask you a question about Grayton."

The man crossed his arms over his well-fed belly. "Go right ahead."

Nate prayed his instincts and his silver tongue were working today. "I represent a group, D.H. Enterprises, and we are new to the town. We are looking for upstanding citizens like you to offer our services to."

One silver eyebrow arched. "Services?"

"Anything that needs to be done, we can do. Our skills run far and wide and our willingness knows no bounds."

Nate's stomach cramped and he knew it was about to yowl like an old hound dog. He tightened his muscles and willed it to shut up.

"Is that so?"

"Absolutely. I was on my way into the store to ask the proprietor if he wouldn't mind posting an advertisement for us."

"What do you want from me?" The stranger's gaze hadn't changed from icy. Nate hoped he could melt at least a drop or two off.

"Do you know if there are any ranchers or citizens like yourself who might be in need of...services?"

Oh, hell, I sound desperate, even to my ears.

The man, Nate still didn't know his name dammit, stroked his chin with one hand. "I'll keep it in mind. You go on in and tell Marvin I told you it was okay to post your advertisement in the store."

He started to walk past Nate with a nod. It was now or never.

"It was a pleasure to meet you..."

"Persistent little shit, ain't ya?" He threw back his head and laughed a loud booming guffaw that nearly made the bell ring in the store. "I like that. Samuel O'Shea." He finally held out his hand and Nate shook it, surprised to find the older man had a grip like a bear trap.

"Thank you, sir. I hope we can do business together."

"We just might," O'Shea said and walked away toward the saloon Nate had spotted on the way into town.

Nate's stomach grumbled, but he ignored it and with a grin, headed into the store.

Elisa Taggert stood in the corner of the store with her fists clenched. She told herself to relax and take a breath, but it was hard. So hard. What she really wanted to do was follow Samuel O'Shea out that door and put a bullet in him. Or two.

Bastard.

He dared pretend he hardly knew her, or that he hadn't stolen her father's land right out from under him. O'Shea treated her like a goddamn stranger!

The bell tinkled over the door and a man walked in. Elisa judged him to be in his mid-twenties, with dark hair settled under a dark brown hat. Gray trousers marked him as an ex-Confederate soldier, although his jacket was of good quality. Elisa noted the bulge of a gun on his left hip. Wide shoulders filled out the jacket nicely. His fingers were long and twitched as if he needed to be moving constantly.

His gaze swung to hers and she could see the hunter within him. The moment his dark eyes touched hers, she felt a jolt go through her from top to bottom. Her heart started pounding and her palms grew moist. Actually, to her shame, they weren't the only moist part of her body.

Sweet Mary, he was beautiful. A sharp chin with an outline of whiskers framing the deep cleft in the middle. A long, aristocratic nose sat between the darkest, deepest eyes she'd ever seen. Eyes that knew pain, misery and perhaps joy. Elisa's entire world shifted slightly under her booted feet and she knew an eternal moment of uncertainty.

Who was he?

He blinked and the spell between them snapped. She stepped further into the shadows of the corner and he paused before walking to the counter to talk to Marvin. Elisa pressed her hand to her chest to push on her racing heart. What the hell was wrong with her? A handsome stranger glanced at her and she turned into a blithering, foolish woman?

"Good afternoon, sir. Nate Marchand at your service. I was wondering if you wouldn't mind posting this advertisement in your store."

His voice was like hot honey on a biscuit, warm and smooth. A shiver licked up her spine at the southern drawl and the gentlemanly tone. Most definitely a southerner, likely from Alabama or Georgia. There were plenty of them in Texas—like ragweed, they just kept popping up.

"Advertisement for what?" Marvin asked. He was one of those people she wasn't sure was for her or against her. She'd known Marvin nearly all her life, but he refused to take a side in the battle for her father's land. That landed him square in her suspicious group of folks.

Elisa walked toward the shelf of canned peaches to peek through at the two men. The stranger stood at least a head taller than Marvin, who was a short, balding man with barely enough shoulder to shrug. His watery eyes hid behind thick spectacles. Then he did the one thing that really irked her—he licked his finger to wipe down his eyebrows, which seemed to have a life of their own, wiry little buggers.

"D.H. Enterprises. We're new to town and we'd like to advertise our services."

Oh, God, that voice. It was wreaking havoc on Elisa's equilibrium. Every time he spoke, another bolt of awareness ripped through her. It was disconcerting and downright annoying. She didn't know this stranger from a hole in the ground. Why should he affect her so strongly?

"What kind of services?"

A minute sigh drifted from the stranger's mouth and she sensed his frustration at repeating the same information. Likely in every town he and his "Enterprises" had passed through.

"Anything that needs to be done. My colleagues and I are available immediately."

"Well, I dunno, stranger," Marvin hedged. "Sounds a mite bit shady to me."

"Mr. O'Shea told me to tell you it was okay to post it."

The stranger's words rippled around her and anger replaced her fascination with him.

"What business do you have with Mr. O'Shea?" she snapped as she stepped out into full view.

Marvin's eyebrows went clear to his hairline and he skittered backwards like a bug.

The stranger turned toward her and his dark gaze swept her up and down. Noted the trousers, the old, faded calico shirt, the dirty neckerchief and scuffed chaps. Not to mention the battered hat that sat on her head with a big hole through the center of it. Her damned body betrayed her by warming to the touch of his gaze. She tried to clench her muscles and will away the feelings, but it was no use. She was aroused, dammit to hell.

"Ma'am." He tipped his hat. Elisa caught a glimpse of dark, wavy hair that looked as soft as satin. "Mr. O'Shea is a prospective client."

That did it. She stomped forward until she was nearly nose to nose with him, well, nose to chin anyway.

"That makes you an enemy of mine. Anyone who does business with that son of a bitch deserves what they get. More than likely a bullet in the back and empty pockets." Elisa glanced at Marvin. "Let me know when that new tack comes in, Marvin."

The older man nodded, his gaze swinging back and forth like a clock pendulum between Elisa and the stranger.

"Strong words, ma'am," the stranger said. "I don't rightly know what put the bee in your bonnet, but I don't believe I am anyone's enemy in Grayton."

Grayton. A town named after her grandfather. A town that allowed the largest landowner in the county to steal the land her grandfather had rightly claimed fifty years ago.

"Wrong." Elisa turned and headed toward the door. One strong hand clamped on her arm, stopping her exit, and almost stopping her heart. She thought meeting his gaze gave her body a shock. Touching him nearly gave her apoplexy.

"Let go of me," she ground out through clenched teeth, hoping the baggy shirt hid the telltale peaks of her nipples. She had the crazy notion of grabbing him and kissing him until neither one of them could see straight.

"Pardon me," he said as he released her arm. "I just wanted to tell you that I'm sorry you believe I'm your enemy. Far from it. My name is Nathaniel Marchand. My friends call me Nate."

Nathaniel Marchand. Nate.

"And you are?"

Elisa realized she stood there staring into his bottomless black eyes and hadn't responded to his introduction or his apology. She cursed her freckled complexion and hoped a flush hadn't crept up her cheeks.

"No friend of that bastard O'Shea. I'll tell you this, Mr. Marchand. If you do business with him, you are definitely my enemy."

With that, she forced her feet to keep walking out the door and back to the ranch. She didn't trust herself. Mr. Marchand was like a box of chocolates she wanted to savor, bite by bite, but if he was in business with O'Shea, she'd do well to keep her mouth to herself.

Nate watched the young woman leave the store and with great effort resisted the urge to chase after her. Holy hell, just the sight of her had affected him like nothing he'd ever felt before. She wasn't classically beautiful, or even clean for that matter, but there was something...elemental about her that made his dick stand at attention and his balls heavy with need. Her intelligence and wit were obvious, and as sharp as that tongue of hers.

"Who was that?" he asked the older man.

"Elisa Taggert. 'Twas her granddaddy, Jed Grayton, who started this town from a patch of dirt in the middle of nowhere. He brought the first head of cattle out here and set up his ranch."

Elisa. The name fit her Irish beauty perfectly. The pert freckled nose, the deep blue eyes that practically shot sparks at him, and those lips. Hell, he was going to dream about those pink lips for the rest of his life. They were plump and pouty by nature—the kind that made him want to nibble and lick for hours. He shifted in his trousers, hoping Marvin didn't notice the erection currently pulsing between his legs. Damn that little hellion.

"O'Shea said you could set up that advertisement?"

Nate shook his head to clear it. The fiery woman in the trousers had not only confused his body, she'd confused his mind. He'd even forgotten he was hungry.

"Yes, he did. Would it be acceptable to hang it in the window?"

Marvin shrugged. "'S okay, I suppose. Where should I send folks if they ask about you?"

"Just outside town near the clearing with the small stream. Do you know it?"

Marvin nodded. "Yep, sure do. Let's get your paper hung up then."

Within moments, the D.H. Enterprises advertisement that Nate had painstakingly made five copies of was hung. He only hoped that business would come along sooner than later. His stomach picked that particular moment to remind him how empty it was. After the cramp passed, he turned to shake Marvin's hand.

"Do you need any supplies out there, Mr. Marchand? Any friend of O'Shea's..."

Nate wanted to say no, but dammit to hell, he was so fucking hungry. Buying on credit was not a good idea, but he figured he could work it off, if necessary.

"Actually, we do, Marvin." He rattled off a list of supplies that included coffee, something he'd probably sell his right foot for, and staples to make five men reasonable meals for two weeks. Just like that, he had the supplies and was out the door.

Nate glanced at the advertisement and smiled. Grayton was going to be the turning point for D. H. Enterprises. He could feel it in his bones, bones that would soon be fed well for the first time in months.

Chapter Two

Elisa jumped on her Arabian, Midnight, and rode out of town like her hair was on fire. The deep thunder of the horse's hooves echoed through her body, soothing her. She'd always struggled with her temper, her impatience. This time she was impatient with herself.

The wind whistled past her ears as the late spring warmth coated her face.

For some unknown reason the stranger, Nate, had affected her like no other. That alone made her angry. The fact that he considered himself available to work for O'Shea made it worse.

Her mother's gentleness had always helped during Elisa's spells of fury. With her mother gone the last year, Elisa struggled almost daily with her inner devils. At the moment, they were jumping up and down on her back cackling madly.

Damn idiot. Life wasn't complicated enough, now she had to go and get herself twisted up over a stranger. A man. Elisa's contact with men had been limited to cowboys and her family. Of course, her father and brother didn't count. Cowboys treated her like one of them. She'd never even once had time to think of a man as anything other than a person.

A man complicated life too much and it was already complicated enough. Elisa would have to avoid Nate. With her work at home it wouldn't be too hard. Every waking moment was spent trying to keep the Taggert ranch running.

She passed the walnut tree that marked the edge of their property. Her tension lessened somewhat but her temper still simmered. Elisa eased up on Midnight and slowed him to a trot. As the horse breathed slower so did she. They calmed down together. By the time she reached the house, she felt more in control of her emotions.

As much control as she could have anyway. She found her father sitting on the porch where she'd left him, whittling a piece of wood and staring into his knife as if it held the keys to the world.

"Da, why are you still sitting there? You were supposed to relieve Daniel an hour ago." She dismounted and stopped herself from shaking him. A deep breath of the sticky air did nothing to alleviate the smell of failure. The failure of the Taggert ranch and the end of their family history.

"What was that?" He looked up. The breeze ruffled his dark brown hair liberally sprinkled with gray, and his normally sharp green eyes softened with confusion.

"Daniel. You were supposed to relieve Daniel so he could have some time to sleep. He's been up all night watching the herd, Da." She threw her gloves on the ground. "And that damned Marvin forgot to order the tack for us. I think he's about to stop our credit at the store."

"Don't curse, darlin'. 'Tis not fitting for a lady." Her father continued to whittle away at the piece of wood that didn't resemble anything but a piece of whittled wood.

"Lady?" she snorted. "Who the hell are you talking to? I haven't been a lady since I was fifteen years old and had to run this ranch. Goddammit, between you and Ma—"

She never even saw him move, but he slapped her so hard, her ears rang. Elisa knew her father still had strength and speed, but it had been so long since he'd done anything but mope, she'd doubted its existence.

"Don't you dare speak of your sainted mother when you're blaspheming." He shook with rage, his pale face suddenly florid. "I'll thank you to keep a civil tongue in your mouth. I'm still the owner of this ranch and your father."

"Then act like it."

"How dare you."

"I've dared a lot of things, Da. If I hadn't, you'd be sitting in an alley eating scraps for meals. We've got to save this ranch and we can't do it if you are still grieving. It's been a year already." Her voice cracked on the last word. It had been a hard three years, but the last had nearly broken her spirit.

Her father simply stared, his eyes brimming with unshed tears. His mouth opened and closed, but he didn't respond. Instead, he sat back down on the stump and started whittling again.

Anger and frustration roared through Elisa. She couldn't be near him much anymore without the urge to rage. It wouldn't help matters any, so she spent as much time as possible away from her father.

With a deep breath, she mumbled, "I'll go relieve him then."

She threw herself back on Midnight and rode off toward Daniel. At least watching the herd would give her relief from her family. God knows she needed more than relief. She needed a miracle.

୫୦୯୫

When Nate arrived back at camp, the rest of the Devils were sitting around the campfire staring glumly at what appeared to be a squirrel roasting above the flames. He hid a grin at the scowl on Lee's face.

Gideon looked up and nodded. "Hey there, Nate. Glad you're back. I sure as hell hope you found a deer or something on the way."

"I had a bit of success in town actually." He dismounted and revealed the bulging pack of supplies strapped to the back of his horse.

"Holy shit," Jake said with a grin.

"A bit of success? Shit, you idiot, that's more than a bit of anything." Lee's eyes widened at the sight of the food.

Nate couldn't be bothered to get angry at the sourpuss. Instead, he untied the pack and handed it to Zeke, already standing at his side. The blond man took the supplies and walked back to the campfire. Lee tried to snatch it from him, but with a roll and a twist, Zeke moved from the one-armed man's grasp.

"Bastard."

"Nope, our parents were married, little brother." Zeke set the pack down by Gideon.

Funny how the easygoing Gideon had become their leader. He hadn't asked for it, it came by him naturally. They'd all unofficially adopted him as the man in charge, even after the war. It spoke volumes that Zeke handed the food over to his cousin Gideon without a word.

"Where did you get these, Nate?" Gideon's quiet question made them all pause.

"In town at the store." Nate started unsaddling Bonne Chance, knowing that Gid would not approve of buying supplies with nothing to pay for them.

"How did you get them?"

"I ran into a man in town named O'Shea. He's a big man in Grayton. After conversing with him, I was able to hang our advertisement in the store. The proprietor"—he swallowed—"allowed me to purchase some food stuffs on credit."

"On credit? What does that mean?" Lee demanded.

"It means he gave his word he'd pay for them, but no money changed hands."

"That's okay, Gid," Jake piped up. "We can't work if we don't eat. Better than what I was planning on doing later." He raised on auburn eyebrow at Nate, then winked.

"I don't think it's okay. With Captain Nessman dogging our tail, we don't need to leave a debt behind we can't pay." Gideon eyed the burlap wrapped sack with unease on his face.

"Fuck Nessman," Lee snapped. "I'm tired of living my life wondering if that Yankee is going to arrest us for being ex-Confederate soldiers. If that dick has nothing else to do then I say fuck him."

Gideon frowned at Lee. "We haven't seen Nessman in almost a month. He's not what we're talking about."

"I don't care if it's been a month or six months. Nessman is ghosting us, Gid." Lee scratched at the stump of his arm. "Ol' fancy pants is getting us knee-deep in shit."

Nate's good mood started to fade. "I got us some food. We're starving, Lee, not living high off the hog. Gid, it's not chocolate and cigars. It's flour, coffee and bacon."

"Did you say bacon?" Jake eyed the bundle even closer.

Gideon looked at Zeke. "What do you think?"

Zeke followed Jake's gaze then glanced at Lee. "Lee's got a point about Nessman. Gid's right about promising money we don't have for food." His gaze turned to Nate. "But I think Nate did the right thing. We are starving and even if we have to work it off for the store owner, we needed food."

Nate breathed an inner sigh of relief. At least Zeke and Jake agreed with him, and that was three out of five. Lee leveled a dirty look at Nate, but he didn't respond in kind. Nate's stomach actually hurt from being empty for so long and from the constant bickering.

"How about we have some biscuits and beans?"

His simple suggestion seemed to take the edge off everyone's anger. Zeke went to get water while Jake stoked up the fire. Gideon examined everything in the sack carefully as if gauging the worthiness of the purchase. Nothing Nate had brought back was frivolous—a word that did not exist in Nate's world anyway.

When Gideon finished looking at the supplies, he nodded at Nate. It was an approval and Nate finally breathed normally. The last thing he wanted to do was alienate anyone in his family, something the ragtag Devils had become.

After they filled their bellies for the first time in weeks, Zeke and Jake went off to hunt, while Gideon, Lee and Nate cleaned their tack.

Gideon broke the silence. "What was this man O'Shea like?"

Nate pursed his lips. "Big, loud, dangerous."

Gideon nodded. "I know the type. What about his clothes?"

"Expensive, down to the boots."

"You would notice that," Lee interjected.

"We have to find someone who can pay us, Lee. Would you rather work for someone as poor as we are?" Gideon shook his head. "Can you just listen for now? We'll need you if we're going to be successful."

Lee frowned. "Fine."

"Tell me everything you remember."

Nate searched his memory. "The shopkeeper respected him, gave me the food based solely on mention of O'Shea's name. He was a weasel, but easily manipulated." The image of the woman flashed through his mind. "I expect O'Shea is the kind of man who has a lot of enemies, someone who might need extra protection."

"Money, power and a small town. I'd say you're right on target. O'Shea is definitely the man to work for. Anything else?" Gideon's sharp gaze probed Nate's.

"There was a woman there. She, ah, didn't appear to be pleased that I even knew O'Shea." Nate swallowed. "She was dressed in clothes that looked worse than ours. I don't think she'll be a problem."

The words fell between them ringing false like a cracked bell.

"I trust your judgment. It's a good thing too because we've got a rider coming."

All three of them stood at the ready with hands resting on pistols. Like the good soldiers they had been, Lee and Nate flanked Gideon, every nerve stretched tight. A sense of calm settled over Nate and he breathed evenly, deeply.

The rider was alone, coming toward them at a steady pace on a big bay. He stopped and dismounted fifteen feet away. A tall, lanky man with a pair of well-used pistols resting on his hips, he tipped his hat back revealing jet black hair and equally dark eyes.

"Keep an eye on his right hand." Gideon's mouth barely moved.

"Hello the camp." The stranger raised his left hand and waved, a smile on his face.

"What can we do for you?" Gideon replied.

Although the stranger didn't do anything that could be construed as threatening, Nate had an itch on the back of his neck. The man had more on his mind than friendly conversation.

"Y'all are D.H. Enterprises?"

"That's right," Gideon responded for them.

Nate felt a trickle of sweat slide down his back as the Texas heat settled on them like a hot blanket.

"Mr. O'Shea sent me over to invite you for supper. He has a business proposition for you." The stranger wiped his hand under his nose. "I see you've settled in nicely here. This here is O'Shea's land and he'd like to offer you the use of it while you're in town." Another smile spread across his face.

"That's right friendly of him," Lee said with his usual brand of sarcasm.

Gideon quelled his cousin with one glance, then looked back toward the stranger. "We'd be honored to join Mr. O'Shea for supper. Three of us will come."

The stranger's gaze swept the area. "There's more than three of you then?"

"Yes."

Nate knew Gideon was not about to reveal their exact numbers yet.

"Just head due north, you'll find O'Shea's ranch in about half an hour. Be there at six o'clock." The stranger mounted his horse again.

"Your name, sir?"

The grin seemed genuine. "You can call me Rodrigo. I am Mr. O'Shea's foreman."

"My thanks for coming by. Name's Gideon. This is Nate and Lee."

Rodrigo tipped his hat. "Pleased to meet you. Welcome to Grayton, fellas." With another wave, he rode back from the direction he came.

Nate let out his breath slowly and looked at Gideon, who raised one eyebrow.

"I'm guessing O'Shea has more men working for him worse than Rodrigo. He's probably the welcoming committee. You sure about this?"

"I'm sure O'Shea has money and I'm also sure we can't survive another month without some." Nate probably wouldn't have spoken to a man like O'Shea prior to the war. None of them would have, but times had changed. Life had changed. It was time to change with it.

⁎⁎⁎

By five-fifteen, Zeke, Gideon and Nate were ready to leave. Lee was not happy about staying behind with Jake.

"You're not letting me go because you want men with two good arms to go with you, right?"

"That's a load of shit, Lee. I'm not taking you because you're a hothead. I don't want our first business meeting with O'Shea to end with you and your rebel yell." Gideon didn't get mad often, but when pushed, his voice and his will turned to steel. "None of us care if you only have one arm, so why the hell do you?"

The silence grew uncomfortable as the cousins stared each other down. Jake, as was his usual style, broke the tension.

"Well, hell, with Lee having only one arm, that just means I can beat him at tug of war." Jake winked at Lee. "And, he never has to wash the damn dishes."

"Idiot." Lee's lips twitched.

"Moron." Jake grinned so widely, they laughed and even Lee cracked a smile.

"Let's mount up and head over there. Wouldn't do for us to be late for our first meeting." Nate hated to be late, being punctual was the sign of a gentleman. He wanted so badly to hang onto the small things like that which made life bearable.

Zeke shook his head and Gideon clapped him on the shoulder.

"Let's go then." Gideon chuckled.

They mounted up and rode across the Texas prairie toward their future. If they somehow lost the opportunity to work for O'Shea, the Devils were in serious trouble. From what Nate surmised, O'Shea was not only powerful in Grayton, but likely in the entire county. It was critical that they make a good first impression and do all they could to garner his favor.

Nate kept a close eye on everything around them. Wouldn't surprise him at all if Rodrigo or someone just like him planned a welcoming party. Fifteen minutes into their ride, movement in the trees on the right caught his attention. He whistled quickly under his breath and indicated the trees to Gideon. Zeke broke left, Nate headed straight, while Gideon went right.

The rider burst from the trees, startling a flock of quail. Nate cut off the stranger's escape and yanked Bonne Chance's reins hard enough that he raised his hooves. Predictably, the other horse shied from the war-trained sorrel's offense. Nate launched himself at the off-balance rider and they both tumbled to the ground.

A solid fist landed in his diaphragm, stealing his breath. Nate held on, rolling along the grassy ground, fighting for his life. Punching, snarling and grunting, the two of them were locked in combat until he found himself beneath the stranger and the unmistakable nose of a pistol pressing into his balls.

"One more punch and I'll pull the trigger."

The voice was familiar, *very* familiar.

"Elisa?"

She scrambled off him, breathing heavily. "What the hell are you doing attacking me?"

"I wasn't the one sneaking around in the trees," Nate snapped, all too aware of how her body felt on top of his. Unwelcome and licentious thoughts whooshed through his brain. Jesus, she was all woman, all over, regardless of her clothes or the dirt on her face.

"I wasn't sneaking. This happens to be my land." She holstered the pistol and put her hands on her hips.

"Anything you need help with, Nate?" Gideon asked from behind them.

Elisa's head snapped up and she glared at the other two men. "I suppose these are your friends."

"Yes, they are. Gideon and Zeke Blackwood, this is Elisa Taggert." He stood, wiping the dirt off his pants.

"Ma'am." Gideon tipped his hat.

"Ma'am." Zeke simply nodded.

She returned the nod, but continued to glare at Nate. "Happy to meet you, fellas."

Nate tried to find the right words to apologize. "We were on our way to an appointment. I, ah, apologize for the mix-up. I certainly didn't mean to assault your person."

One eyebrow shot up. "You sure do talk fancy."

"I treat all ladies with respect, ma'am."

She laughed, a husky sound that echoed through him. "Sure as hell ain't talking to a lady, but I'll take your respect since you're standing on my property."

Zeke and Gideon mounted up and waited. Nate stared at Elisa, almost overcome by the urge to kiss her pouty pink lips. He could still feel the press of her breasts on his chest, the memory of them would likely be embedded there for weeks. Dammit.

"Are you leaving or you gonna stand there and stare at me all day?" She frowned.

"My a-apologies, Miss Taggert. We'll be on our way." He picked up his hat and nodded to her, too embarrassed to do more. Just the fact that he'd punched her was enough to make him stammer like an idiot.

Her blue eyes nearly bored holes into him as her right hand rested on the pistol strapped to her nicely curved hip. He hadn't really known how curvy she was until he'd decided to tackle her. As it was, he had trouble remembering what the hell he was doing before Elisa's horse caught his eye. Life as he knew it had changed so much so fast and now it just changed again. Drastically.

As they rode off, Nate could feel Elisa's gaze locked on him and he hoped like hell he didn't run into her any time soon. She was the kind of woman who could make him lose control. That situation must never happen. Nate kept a leash on his sanity with an iron grip.

Elisa stood in the shadows, watching the men ride away. Her heart seemed about to burst from her chest it beat so hard. She'd never touched a man before, not a real man anyway, much less get into a tussle with one. A tussle that made her blood race and every last bit of her come to life. Even her heart.

She knew Nate Marchand was going to be trouble, which is why she'd told herself to avoid him. Yet there he was on her property and instead of doing the smart thing and simply ignoring him and his friends, she followed them. Along with the men who were following Nate. She'd noticed them immediately and thanks to Nate, they knew of her presence.

Midnight seemed to sense her unease, because he pranced around beneath her, whinnying softly. Elisa took deep breaths, yet her body still hummed. Nate and his friends were heading toward O'Shea's ranch. That meant he was definitely not for her.

Now if only she could convince her body of that fact.

"Was that the woman?"

Nate started. "Huh?"

"Was that her? The woman you said wouldn't be any trouble?" Gideon's voice held just a trace of amusement.

"Yes, that was her."

"Hm, no trouble? I think that's already not true." Gideon smiled at Zeke. "What about you, Ezekiel?"

"I think if you call me that again, I'll have to punch you." He glanced at Nate. "But as far as Romeo goes here, oh yeah, big trouble."

Gideon and Zeke both chuckled, shooting sidelong winks at Nate.

"Oh shut up, both of you. I didn't come here to Grayton to find a woman. You know that. I, uh, certainly didn't mean to get into a fistfight with her." Nate shifted uncomfortably on his saddle.

Gideon laughed so suddenly, Nate couldn't help but laugh with him, then remembered why he was laughing.

"It's not funny."

"Oh yes it is." Gideon smiled. "It feels too good to laugh about romance again, Nate. Long time since any of us have had a sweetheart."

"She's *not* my sweetheart. For God's sake, she probably hasn't bathed in a week." Nate felt guilty for even saying that out loud. It wasn't true and it was downright mean to boot. "I mean, she's not my sweetheart. She's just a w-woman."

"A beautiful redhead," Zeke mused.

"Leave her alone, Zeke." The words burst from Nate's mouth like a gunshot.

Gideon and Zeke looked at each other and smiled.

"No trouble at all. Nope, not even a smidge." Gideon tried to smother a smile with his hand.

"Let's pick up the pace so we're not late for our appointment," Nate snapped, desperate to change the subject, to get his mind off Elisa Taggert and what she did to him.

"Yes, sir." Gideon saluted Nate and it was so ridiculous, all three of them laughed.

Nate's mind kept drifting back to Elisa, so he forced himself to focus on the horizon and reaching O'Shea's ranch without anything else happening. Gideon and Zeke kept Nate between them, constantly scanning, watching. During the war, Zeke had been their planner, the one who created and executed raids with amazing precision. Nothing had changed there. Gideon still looked to him.

"Anybody watching?" Gideon asked quietly.

"At least two of them, but I'm thinking there's a third." Zeke shifted and unsnapped the leather on his holster. "They've been tracking us for at least five miles."

"Any threat?" Nate swallowed hard. He was hoping he'd never have to hear the sound of battle again. Hoping, of course, never got him anything. If he never heard a cannonball whistling through the air again, he'd die a happy man.

"Some, but I think they've been ordered to just watch." Zeke gestured to their right. "They could have picked us off if they wanted to."

Nate felt the familiar tickle of danger on his back and freed his own weapon. He saw Gideon do the same. No doubt the men watching them knew the Devils were not inexperienced fools. By the time they reached the gates to the O'Shea ranch house, the tension had only increased. Nate was glad they'd left Lee behind. Damn fool would've ridden straight toward the men watching them, more than likely screaming like a lunatic.

Two armed men at the gate nodded as they passed by. When they reached the front porch, two men emerged from the shadows of the late day sun, O'Shea and Rodrigo.

It was the biggest house Nate had seen since leaving Georgia. A palatial mansion by most standards with Doric columns, acres of windows and even a balcony out on the second story. All in perfect condition with nary a paint chip in sight.

"Evenin', gentlemen." O'Shea's steely gaze swept over them. "I'm glad you were able to accept my invitation."

"Thank you for the invitation, sir." Nate tipped his hat, then dismounted and gestured to the others. "May I present my associates, Gideon and Zeke Blackwood."

"Brothers?"

"Cousins." Gideon dismounted and held out his hand to O'Shea. "Pleasure to meet you, Mr. O'Shea."

Zeke followed suit and stood to Gideon's left, his gaze soaking in everything he saw. No doubt tucking it away in that clever brain of his.

O'Shea shook Gideon's hand, and a small battle of wills ensued. Nate could see the grip between them neared the point of breaking bones.

"Well, what do you say we sit down and get acquainted?" Gideon gestured to the ranch around them, bustling with prime horseflesh, dozens of cowboys and a few Mexican women hanging wash. "This ranch is beautiful."

O'Shea finally let loose his death grip on Gideon's hand. "Thank you, Mr. Blackwood. I've worked hard to get what I have and aim to keep it."

"I know what it means to lose what you love, so I fully appreciate the sentiment, Mr. O'Shea." Nate smiled his winningest smile and stepped up to the porch.

"Let's go inside and have a bit of whiskey. I think you boys might be just what I've been looking for."

As Nate followed O'Shea into the house, he couldn't stop the shiver of unease that crept up his spine. He reminded himself that food and fact were more important than feelings.

ဆြၺ

"What do you mean, remove the Taggerts?" Nate thought perhaps he hadn't heard correctly.

"They're squatting on my land. Land I purchased fair and square a year ago." O'Shea took a drag from the fat cigar in his hand. "That daughter of Sean's is a stubborn little thing, thinks she has a right to it since her granddaddy founded the town. Every time we tell them to leave, she takes a shot at us."

The four of them sat in a living room on more expensive furniture than they'd seen since before the war. Fresh-squeezed lemonade had been placed before them on a shiny wooden table, virtually untouched. Nate probably couldn't drink it if he tried. As it was, he was having trouble keeping the food down they'd eaten earlier.

Nate swallowed hard. "So you want to hire us to remove them? Exactly how?"

"That ain't my problem. You see, I've tried everything I can but they won't leave." O'Shea stretched his legs out and shifted in the leather chair he occupied. "That's where you come in. You remove the Taggerts, I pay you five hundred dollars."

"Each," Zeke interjected. "Plus a fifty dollar advance."

"I wondered when you'd speak, Mr. Blackwood. You're the quiet one in the bunch, ain't ya?" O'Shea took a gulp of his lemonade. "Each, eh? How many of you are there in D.H. Enterprises?"

Gideon met Nate's gaze for a moment before turning to O'Shea. "There are five of us. If we take this job, we want certain assurances."

O'Shea's steely eyes narrowed. "What kind of assurances?"

"My guess is that you are, shall we say, friends with the local law enforcement. If we have to employ certain tactics to remove the Taggerts, I want your assurances that we won't spend any time in jail." Gideon's tone brooked no argument on that point.

Nate's entire body broke out in a sweat. Gideon was already talking about what they'd have to do, illegal or not, to the Taggerts. Fact was, they had to take this job, regardless of how he felt personally. Nate had to forget his fascination with the exasperating Elisa and grab what life was offering. A chance.

"I insist on putting the agreement in writing, as well. No offense to you, Mr. O'Shea, but as a businessman, I'm sure you understand." Nate gulped a bit of lemonade to unlock his throat.

O'Shea puffed the cigar again. "I didn't know what to expect from you, Mr. Marchand, and I'm pleased to find that you are a smart man."

"Thank you kindly, Mr. O'Shea. Now about the fee." He glanced at Zeke. "As Mr. Blackwood says, it's five hundred each, for a total of two thousand five hundred dollars, plus any supplies we might need. In return, we shall remove the Taggerts within one month's time." Nate held out his hand. "Do we have an agreement?"

O'Shea regarded them for a long, silent moment. Nate stepped on the small part of him that protested the thought of forcing Elisa off her property. O'Shea had shown them the bill of sale signed by her mother. If she refused to leave, then she left herself open to be moved by any means necessary.

"We have an agreement. Five hundred dollars each with a fifty dollar advance."

O'Shea shook Nate's hand. The coldness of his skin was not lost on Nate.

D.H. Enterprises finally had a paying job.

Chapter Three

Lee was practically hopping like a jackrabbit by the time they made it back to camp. Gideon had the forethought to ask the cook for enough of the delicious chicken dinner to feed two men. Jake smiled and dug in with gusto, not even bothering to ask questions. Lee had other ideas.

Before they even unsaddled the horses, he peppered them with questions.

"What's the job? What does it pay? Are we working for O'Shea? Did you take it? What the hell happened? Isn't anyone going to tell me?" His brown eyes snapped in the firelight.

"I would if you'd stop talking for five seconds," Zeke groused. "Sit down and eat, Lee. We'll be right there."

"Don't think you can order me around. I might be younger but I'm—"

"Sit down and eat." Gideon touched Lee's right shoulder. "It's really good chicken and the biscuits remind me of your mama's."

That seemed to take the air out of Lee's anger. He shrugged off Gideon's hand and walked over to Jake. When he sat down, Jake handed him a chicken leg with a smile. Lee stared at them intently while they took care of the horses, looking as if he wanted to shake the story out of them.

Nate knew the morning would bring the first real day of their job and he wanted an evening of quiet. Lee probably wouldn't let that happen. As Gideon and Zeke headed to the fire, Nate walked off toward the stream alone.

"I'll be back in a few minutes."

He heard Lee curse and Gideon's quiet murmur. No doubt Gid would be able to tell them the entire story without Nate's help anyway. There wasn't that much to tell. The Devils had to remove a young woman, her crippled father and younger brother from the land O'Shea claimed was his. The Taggerts only had about two hundred head of cattle left. O'Shea said they'd had to sell off most of it to survive.

How hard could it be to remove them?

Elisa watched as the man walked toward the stream, knowing it was Nate without even seeing his face. He had a way about him that was recognizable in the moonlight. When he reached the stream, he sighed as he lay back on the grass with his knees up and his arms folded behind his head.

She crept closer, careful not to disturb any of the foliage around her. If Elisa was good at anything, it was being stealthy. She'd had to become a hunter to feed her brother and mother while Da had been off to war. They'd had plenty of meat those two years.

When she was within a few yards, she could see his face quite clearly in the light of the moon. His expression seemed contemplative, almost melancholy. She wondered what he was thinking about—probably how much money he'd make working for O'Shea. Dirty, rotten stinker.

Before he could sense her nearby, she pounced. She pinned his elbows down with her knees, slapped a hand across his mouth as her knife rested comfortably on his throat. The scent of man and of Nate wafted up at her, tickling her nose and her sleeping arousal.

"I see you had a nice visit with that bastard," she hissed in a whisper. "Did you agree to work for him? Or should I even bother to ask judging from the fried chicken grease on your lips."

He shook his head, wiggling beneath her, but Elisa was no featherweight. She held him down securely.

"If I lift my hand, will you promise not to yell for your friends?"

Nate's eyes narrowed but he nodded against her hand. When she lifted it, he growled at her. *Growled!*

"What do you think you're doing?"

"Trying to figure out what you were doing at O'Shea's." No need to lie to the man. They both knew where he'd been that day.

"None of your business. Now get off me and I'll let you get away."

She laughed and pressed the knife into his skin a bit more. "I think I have the upper hand here, Johnny Reb."

"It's Nate. Or if you prefer, Nathaniel. I'll even answer to Lieutenant."

"Oh, I touched on a nerve, did I? I'll have to remember that." She pushed down on his elbows, digging them into the hard ground beneath them. "Are you going to tell me what you were doing today?"

"Go to hell."

"Tsk, tsk. Such language and in front of a *lady* too."

Nate jerked his body, almost throwing her off, but Elisa held fast. She nicked his throat, allowing a small drop of blood to well.

"I ain't playing with you, fancy man. You tell me what I want to know or I cut you deeper."

Her blood rushed around so fast, it made her heady. The feeling of power over the big man was intoxicating. Arousing.

"You don't have the heart to do something like that."

"Don't doubt it," she snapped.

Her euphoria pinched by his words, Elisa shifted her knees slightly. That must have been the opportunity he'd been waiting for, because within seconds, their positions were reversed and he pinned her to the ground. The knife landed useless on the ground somewhere behind him.

A rock dug into her back just as his body flattened hers from top to bottom. It was an astounding, startling sensation completely foreign to her. Nate Marchand was no boy. He was a man, all man, with a hard, strong body that had obviously spent a great deal time doing chores. A lot of chores.

"Your turn for listening." His hot breath coated her face with the sweet smell of pipe tobacco. "You have no right to attack me, cut me or try to force me into anything. No one does, do you hear me?"

The sheer fury in his voice scared her. Someone had warned her that soldiers don't take kindly to violence, but she'd shrugged it off. Her mistake.

"I don't answer to you for my actions or my choices. Now when I let you up, you'd best head on home before I turn you over my knee and paddle your ass."

Elisa didn't say a word. She was stuck on the image of Nate spanking her.

"Do you hear me?"

This time instead of speaking, Elisa leaned up and captured his lips in a fierce kiss. Her first actually, giving or receiving, and what a kiss it was. His lips were as hard as the rest of him, unyielding to her assault. She let her instincts guide her and softened the pressure until he relented. Then, heaven shone for a moment in the darkness of a Texas forest.

Sweet delicious kiss. One moment anger, the next the world shifted and Elisa understood what it meant to be alive. His tongue laved her lips, a tickle that she answered by opening her mouth. He invaded like a conqueror, sweeping across her teeth, her tongue, the roof of her mouth. She moaned into his mouth as her nipples hardened, as eager and hungry as the rest of her.

As the pleasure reached a new height, Elisa pushed her pussy upwards, grinding the aching part of her against the obviously aroused part of him. He trembled for just a moment before he ripped his mouth away from hers, breathing ragged as if he'd run a race.

"What the hell was that? Did you think that by offering yourself to me, I'd tell you what you want to know? I don't take advantage of desperate young women, no matter how desperate I am."

When he stood, her body cried out from the loss of heat, from the loss of him. He stalked off downstream, away from her. She was practically vibrating from a million different feelings, none of which she knew the first thing about.

"Go home, little girl. I don't have anything for you."

His raspy voice scratched at her tender ears. Elisa was left in the darkness alone with a throbbing body and an aching heart.

ಬಂಶ

Nate hardly slept a wink. Between Elisa's surprise attack and the job they'd agreed to perform for O'Shea, his brain simply would not stop thinking. It ran through a hundred different plans for how to remove the Taggerts. Unfortunately the rest of him was completely focused on the woman.

Elisa.

God, she'd felt like paradise beneath him. Perfectly formed, Elisa certainly hid a wealth of womanly charms beneath her baggy, manly clothes. Her breasts were full and round with nipples that his chest still remembered vividly, her hips round and curvy with enough to hang on to for the ride.

It would have been the ride of his life if he'd continued even a second longer. As it was, his dick stayed hard for hours until he finally put it to sleep with his hand. Her kiss was inexperienced, but her passion natural.

Nate regretted the entire incident, especially the kiss. Now when they arrived at the Taggerts' door, she had enough ammunition to cut him down at the knees. Dammit. If only she hadn't kissed him, if only he hadn't gone off by himself. If only, if only. He lay there most of the night speaking that phrase over and over in his head. It got him nothing but grainy eyes and a surly disposition.

Even Lee seemed to sense that Nate was not to be fooled with. Everyone steered clear of him, more than likely because he'd barked at them the night before when he made it back to camp.

Gideon appeared to understand. He handed Nate a mug of steaming black coffee and retreated to the other side of the fire.

"Rough night?"

Nate snorted. "You could say that."

"Money hasn't changed hands yet. We can still say no to this job." Gideon's blue eyes were earnest with concern. "I think it's been bothering you since you shook hands with O'Shea."

Gideon was, of course, exactly right. It had been bothering Nate, but that wasn't important. Making D.H. Enterprises viable and putting food in their stomachs was.

"We can't say no, Gid. Not unless we want to starve." He glanced at Zeke and Lee as they stood in the dewy grass, talking quietly, then at Jake as he fiddled with some kind of contraption on his saddle. "We've come too far, done too much, to stop now. St. Peter may question us when we get to the pearly gates, but for now, we put ourselves first. We're all we've got."

Gideon nodded and took a gulp of his coffee. "I don't disagree with anything you've said, Nate. I'm hungry too and I'm especially worried about Lee. If he doesn't get rid of that chip on his shoulder, he's going to get himself killed. Jake's gonna end up in jail and Zeke will get shot busting him out." He sighed. "You ready to get started today?"

"No, but we're gonna get started anyway." Nate grinned. "Let's fry up some of that bacon and use the soap I brought back so we can start the day with full bellies and sweet-smelling skin."

With a laugh, Gideon reached for the frying pan tucked into his saddlebags. Today would be an important day—everything had to go exactly right.

ಬಿರ

Everything went wrong. In fact, everything that should have gone right, went horribly wrong.

An older man Nate assumed was Sean Taggert sat outside of his home on a chair, whittling. He had graying dark brown hair, and the most haunted green eyes Nate had ever seen. The man glanced up at them, then went back to his whittling, as if he doubted the Devils existed.

"Good morning, sir. Are you Sean Taggert?" Gideon asked.

The old man focused on his handiwork and started mumbling under his breath. The sound of a rifle cocking was the only indication they weren't alone.

"Y'all better have a very good reason for being here," Elisa shouted from somewhere behind them.

"We just want to talk, Miss Taggert." Nate swallowed hard.

"Miss Taggert, is it?" she snorted. "You seem to have a short memory, Mr. Marchand. Your tongue was dancing with mine about twelve hours ago, or don't you remember?"

Gideon looked disappointed. Lee looked murderous. Jake looked impressed while Zeke didn't appear affected at all.

"What the hell does that mean?" Lee hissed. "You were fucking the girl we're supposed to throw off this place?"

"I didn't do anything to her," Nate whispered. "Now shut up a minute, would you?"

"Elisa, can you please come down here and talk to us?" Nate was pleased his voice didn't shake. God knew the rest of him was shaking enough to set Bonne Chance on edge. The sorrel moved restlessly beneath him. He tried unsuccessfully to dislodge the lump in his throat.

A shot pinged off the rock to their left. Every one of the horses stayed put, as battle-trained equine do. However, the Devils all appeared to be ready to attack if one more shot was fired. Nate wished he had the courage to take a drink from his canteen because his mouth had never felt so dry. However, drinking would be a sign of weakness, something he never showed to an enemy. Elisa now fell into the ranks of an enemy.

"Get your sorry asses out of here." Elisa's voice was as sharp as a knife. "Tell O'Shea he can stick that deed up his fat ass. This is Taggert land."

Gideon's mouth pinched in a tight, white line. He stared at Nate, apparently waiting for him to make the decision. Nate wanted to howl in frustration. How could one kiss completely sabotage their first job?

"You know we'll be back, Elisa," he finally ground out. "You can't keep us away forever. We outnumber you, we outgun you and we have unlimited money to fight you. Are you sure you want this?"

She laughed. "I don't give a shit if you have a hundred men with cannons. The only way I'm leaving this land is in a pine box. Now git."

Another rifle shot sounded and the bullet went straight through Nate's hat. It flew through the air and landed by the old man's feet. Grinding his teeth, Nate dismounted. Just as he reached for it, Sean slammed his foot down, grinding it into the mud beneath his boot. Then without a word, he went back to whittling, his boot firmly planted on Nate's now ruined hat.

"Son of a bitch," he cursed under his breath. "Family of lunatics. Can't wait to meet the brother."

Nate nodded at Gideon and the five of them rode back the way they came, empty-handed and angry.

Elisa let out the breath she'd been holding. She watched as Nate and his four large, angry-looking friends rode off. She'd almost had heart palpitations when she saw them looming over Da, who sat there like a bump on a log with five armed men in front of him. He lived in his own world so much, Elisa had been worried about him. Now she was terrified for him. He hadn't been even remotely interested in the men.

A big mistake. A huge one. Elisa assumed the too-handsome Nate worked for O'Shea, so she'd be more prepared to deal with him. If she hadn't been coming back from night watch, Da would have faced them all alone. She and Daniel would have to move the herd even closer than before.

Time to close the ranks and protect themselves. Even if that meant against Nate, the first man to make her heart flutter. Too bad she had to nearly shoot his head off. He'd not likely be forgiving of that particular sin, and she wasn't about to go running into his arms.

She sighed as the five men disappeared on the horizon, then she realized they were headed for the herd—and her fourteen-year-old brother. Eliza leapt to her feet and onto Midnight.

"Hiya! Go, go, go!" She hunkered down low, racing through the trees. She had to beat them to the herd to protect them and Daniel. Branches slapped at her face as she flew past, the cuts stinging and some oozing blood down her cheeks. It didn't matter. None of it mattered except for family.

Elisa burst into the clearing where Daniel sat watching the placid herd. A few lowed at her as she galloped past. He saw her coming and met her halfway across the field. Daniel had the look of their father, with dark brown hair and green eyes, and a build that sat long and lanky on an adolescent body. The promise of a man to come made him appear like a puppy whose paws were too big for its thin body.

"Riders coming. Push the herd back toward the north end of the house. We'll stop them with the cattle they came here to steal."

"Are you sure?" He eyed the fat bovines uncertainly.

"Of course I'm sure. Haven't I taken care of you for the last three years? Listen to me, Daniel Taggert. If you want to save our ranch, our family and our lives, we need to move. *Now.*"

She pulled Midnight around and headed for the right side of the herd and started urging them forward. Luckily, Daniel listened to her and pushed the herd from the left side.

Within five minutes, they were moving at a good pace, not panicked or uncontrollable. A herd of longhorns two hundred head strong was enough to stop anyone. As they rounded the bend near the forest, Elisa caught a glimpse of the five riders in the distance. They reined in their horses and watched as the cattle headed toward them.

Obviously they hadn't dealt much with longhorns or they would've moved immediately. A brief hiccup of guilt surfaced, but Elisa blew it away on the wind. They were playing a deadly game with her family's lives and future, she'd play by the same rules.

"Shit."

"Is that your girlfriend I see pushing a herd of longhorns at us?" Lee scowled at him. "What is she, a demon from the bowels of Hades?"

Nate squirmed in his saddle, wishing he could start the day over again. "Could be. Right now I'd say we need to get out of the way so we don't get trampled by them."

He could see Elisa on one side of the herd, on the other he assumed was her brother. They deliberately moved the cattle to stop the Devils from reaching them or her brother. He'd underestimated Elisa Taggert. She was a sharp opponent. Razor sharp.

The sound of eight hundred hooves moving toward them vibrated in Nate's chest. The sheer power of even such a small herd was not lost on him. He hadn't any experience with large animals except horses and milk cows, nothing like the horned beasts coming straight for them. The rest of his friends appeared as shocked as he was. They turned and galloped away from the cattle.

Nate could almost hear Elisa smiling and his frustration knew no bounds. No doubt the rest of the Devils would let him know how displeased they were with the results of their first day's outing. Nate's stomach roiled and bile crept up his throat. He hated not being in control and if there was anything Elisa did to him, it was threaten his control. Of everything.

"Smart girl," Gideon shouted.

"That's an understatement," Jake piped in. "If you're done with her, Nate, let me know. She's my kind of girl."

"Shut up, fool." Lee shot Jake a dirty look. "Nobody needs to be in that girl's drawers."

"So says you." Jake winked.

"Gid, can I kick his ass?"

"Lee, give it a rest. Geez, can you not be angry for two minutes? Let's swing around back to the house and talk to her father again. At least we know she won't shoot at us while she's busy with the herd." Gideon looked at Nate. "Not an auspicious beginning."

"I realize that. I don't know how things got so... I didn't intend..." He groped for the right words, but couldn't find them. It felt like an army of ants had landed on his skin and were busy biting the hell out of him.

"I know." Gideon glanced back at the herd. "I expect we're not the first men to be confounded by that woman, otherwise O'Shea wouldn't have hired us."

Sounded like the gospel truth to Nate, but it didn't make it any easier to swallow.

They rode back in silence to the house, but when they arrived, the old man was gone. A quick check of the house did not reveal his whereabouts. It seemed that the Taggerts had won the first battle, but the war had just begun.

Chapter Four

When the Devils arrived back at their camp, dirty and beyond frustrated, they had company waiting for them. Unwelcome company.

Captain Elliot Nessman stood next to his thoroughbred horse, his blue Army uniform blinding in the bright sunlight. His narrow face and pointy nose had always reminded Nate of a weasel. Nessman's tactics during their brief imprisonment under his command had solidified that opinion. Although he'd released them after the treaties had been signed, Captain Nessman had made it his God-given duty to put them back behind bars again. Legally or illegally.

Lee cursed under his breath. Gideon shushed him and shot a telling glance to Zeke. Without a word being exchanged, Zeke led Lee toward the stream, away from the volatile situation.

Gideon was the first to break the silence. "Captain Nessman, I didn't know they let your kind into Texas."

"I asked for the duty. You see, it's people like me who will make this country safe from marauders such as yourselves." The crisp Boston accent sounded just plain wrong in the south.

"What business do you have with us, Captain?" Nate didn't think the day could get any worse. Boy how he'd been proved wrong.

"Always the gentleman with manners, eh, Marchand? It just so happens that we had a complaint of squatters 'round here. Look who I found squatting. My favorite group of confederate raiders." He spread his arms. "I'm sure you have permission to be on this land."

"As a matter of fact, we do, Captain. We are under the employ of Mr. Samuel O'Shea. You are more than welcome to confirm that with him at his ranch." Nate pointed to the north. "It's approximately one half hour due north. I'm sure you've heard of Mr. O'Shea."

Nessman's demeanor changed from cocky to angry in the blink of an eye. "I don't believe you."

"That's unfortunate, because it's the truth." Nate felt a certain measure of satisfaction that they'd trumped Nessman's ace.

Nessman threw himself up onto his horse a bit clumsily; the beautiful horse shied and pranced at the movement. "I'm going to confirm your story today. I will be watching you and every movement you make. You step one toe out of line with the law and I'll have you in a federal prison before you know what happened."

"Of that I have no doubt." Gideon watched the captain with a schooled expression.

"You and your Devils on Horseback are bound to break the law sooner or later. It's in your blood," Nessman sneered.

"Just as being an ass is in yours," Jake mused.

"Shut your mouth, you petty thief." Nessman turned his steed toward the north. "You will be seeing me again soon."

Gideon raised one eyebrow. "Thanks for the warning."

With a final nasty look, Nessman rode off into the Texas morning, leaving behind more destruction than he knew.

"What a fantastic morning we've had." Nate dismounted with a leap. "Now all we need is a skunk in camp and the day will be complete."

"I think the skunk just left," Jake quipped.

Gideon and Nate both chuckled, the tension diffused somewhat.

"At least Lee wasn't here to get into a fistfight with him." Nate knew Nessman would throw Lee in jail the moment he swung the first punch.

"Nessman's going to make this job harder than we thought. Especially knowing how hard Elisa Taggert is going to make it." Gideon met Nate's gaze. "We're going to need to discuss strategy."

"I agree. Let's get Zeke and have some dinner."

Like a well-trained troop, they all performed their assigned duties without being asked. Jake got water and made coffee, Lee built up the fire, Zeke prepared the food, Gideon cooked it and Nate distributed it. They'd done it a thousand times before. Now it was done without the urgency, but still with the deliberate actions of soldiers.

The only advantage of how they'd lived the past four years was the way they savored each bite, each experience, each taste of life. When at war, every moment might be the last, so they'd learned to snatch it and hold fast. Nate wondered if there was ever a time when he didn't think the world was mad and he the only sane one in it.

Shaking off his melancholy thoughts, he gave each man their portion of food and coffee. Then it was time to put their heads together, so they talked as they ate, discussing how best to get the Taggerts off their land. Zeke, of course, came up with the best plan of action.

"I have a feeling Miss Taggert has a very big soft spot. We just need to take advantage of it." Zeke nibbled on the ham biscuit. "We need to separate them. The girl's weakness is her family. Once we remove the brother or the father, then she'll be more willing to surrender."

"Surrender? It sounds like a war."

"It is war, Nate. It's us or them. I choose us." Lee stared at him with a dare in his gaze.

"I choose us too which is how we got this job in the first place, Lee. All I'm saying is, before we resort to battle tactics, let's try to talk to them first." Nate didn't want to cause the Taggerts irreparable harm, not even to feed his empty belly.

"We already tried that," Zeke offered. "That girl of yours didn't seem too willing to talk, neither did her bullets."

"She's not my girl."

"So you didn't kiss her?" Jake raised his brows. "You're slipping."

"She kissed me." Nate was getting exasperated. He pulled his collar aside to show them the scab from her little knife trick the night before. "This isn't a love bite. Her knife is as sharp as her mind."

"She cut you?" Gideon examined the wound more closely.

"No, more like tried to get me to talk."

"Hmm, some tactic. Kissing and pricking with a knife. Should've known kissing the prick would've worked." Jake grinned like an idiot.

"Okay, let's focus on the Taggerts, not on my prick."

They all laughed, and Jake nearly knocked over the coffeepot from the hot rock beside the fire.

"Do you think she'll talk to you alone?" Gideon wiped his eyes with his sleeve.

Zeke nodded. "That sounds like a good idea."

Although Nate wanted to argue the point, it *was* a good idea. He and Elisa had a kind of...relationship, for want of a better word. Perhaps she would listen to reason.

∞∞

Nate dismounted half a mile from the house and walked the rest of the way, leading Bonne Chance. He hoped Elisa would see that he meant no harm, particularly since he tied a white cloth to his saddle horn. He'd been running over and over what he was going to say to her, yet it was a jumbled mess of words in his mind.

"You can stop right there, Nate." Her voice, as expected, came from the direction of the trees.

"I just want to talk."

She snorted. "Are you kidding? After the way you showed up at my house this morning and threatened my father?"

That did it.

"For your information, I didn't threaten anyone. You shot at me, ruined my hat, then tried to kill me with your herd of longhorns." Nate didn't get angry often, but when he did, he had a hard time reining it back in. "In fact, you didn't even give me a chance to tell you *why* I was at your house. You simply took it for granted that I was there for nefarious reasons. You've been the aggressor here, Miss Taggert, not me."

Twenty feet ahead, Elisa appeared atop her big black gelding, her rifle pointed at the ground. She licked her lips and cleared her throat.

"So what do you want?"

"Exactly what I wanted earlier. To talk to you." It wasn't a lie at all. He did want to talk—about the Taggerts vacating the land they sat on.

"About what?"

"I'd rather talk, not shout. Do you think you could pick a neutral spot for us to sit down and speak like civilized human beings?"

"Why do you always talk so fancy?" she grumbled.

"My father was a schoolteacher. I chose to take after him and be educated." He hadn't meant to tell her that, but done was done.

"Meet me by the stream near your camp in an hour. We'll talk." She disappeared back into the trees before he could answer.

"Confounded woman." Nate threw himself onto his saddle. "All she does is give orders and shoot at people."

Nate was glad she'd agreed to talk to him. It would be a blessing if the Taggerts agreed to leave without bloodshed. Nate didn't want to be the cause of any more deaths in his lifetime, particularly his own.

Elisa watched as Nate arrived at the stream. For some stupid reason, she considered it their spot since it was the second time they'd met there. It annoyed her that she even thought of it as "their spot" since there was nothing between them.

In broad daylight, there was no hiding how incredibly handsome the Frenchman was. He had thick dark hair that sat in waves on his head, and the blackest eyes she'd seen on a white man. However, what really fascinated her were his hands.

Nate had the most beautiful, graceful hands she'd ever seen, with long fingers and wide palms. Nothing in Elisa's life had been graceful, not even herself. But Nate, when she'd seen his hands move, the word just popped into her mind. It fit him and made her realize that for all the daydreams she'd had of the man, he was far beyond her reach. No graceful, proper-speaking gentleman would ever want a foulmouthed country gal with dirt under her fingernails and calluses on her hands.

She didn't want to startle him, so she rattled the bushes a bit before stepping into the clearing. He glanced at her outfit, but didn't say a word. No doubt comparing her to all the southern belles he'd grown up with.

"So talk." Elisa sat down with her legs criss-crossed and her father's Colt pistol in her hand, cocked and ready. Her knife was strapped to her waist within easy reach.

"Hello to you too."

She waved her hand in the air. "No need for formalities."

"It wasn't a formality. It was courtesy."

"Something a lady would do then?" She narrowed her gaze.

"No, something anyone would do to be polite." He straightened his dark coat and she followed the curve of the fabric across his wide shoulders.

"All right, then, hello, Nathaniel Marchand, my friends call me Nate, but you'll answer to Lieutenant."

When he smiled, it stole her breath. Like a witch's spell, the effect of his beautiful white teeth resonated through her. She hoped to God he couldn't see that her body had grown so rigid, she was afraid she'd shoot herself.

Sweet Mary and all the Saints. Nathaniel Marchand was more than trouble. He was her downfall.

"Hello there yourself, Miss Elisa Taggert. I'm pleased you offered to speak with me this afternoon."

"Uh, yeah, okay." Blithering idiot. She cleared her throat in an effort to rein in her out-of-control body. "What do you want to talk about?"

"As you know, my associates and I have a business, D.H. Enterprises. We were recently hired to assist some folks with relocating their homestead." He pulled at his collar and she saw his Adam's apple bob. "I was hoping you could see your way to, ah, helping us."

Elisa shook her head to blow out the confusion—she had to focus on his fancy talk. "Assist what folks?"

"A family."

She got up on her knees and crawled toward him, the gun heavy in her hand. "What family?"

He glanced at the weapon, then back up at her face. "Ah, a local family."

"That bastard hired you to get rid of us, didn't he? I knew it!" A burst of red ran across her vision. "All this fancy shit of yours and what was it for? To confuse me?"

"No, of course not. I just wanted to t—"

"I'm done talking, Marchand, and I'm sure as hell done listening." She stuck the barrel of the gun against his throat. "You stay the hell off Taggert land or I won't miss that pretty head of yours next time."

"You think my head is pretty?" He blinked rapidly as beads of sweat rolled down his forehead.

"You know you're a handsome man, so don't act all stupid about it. I aim to see how handsome." Elisa's impulses always got the best of her. The urge to see him, all of him, was too much to resist. Her body took over and her mind was powerless to stop it. "Now strip."

"Strip?"

She pushed the barrel deeper into his flesh. "Strip."

He didn't move so she decided to "assist" him. With a wicked grin, she pulled the knife from its scabbard and sliced off two of the buttons from his shirt. The small patch of olive-toned skin made her mouth water. She couldn't wait to see the rest of it.

"I can slice your throat open or shoot you and be away in seconds. Your friends will never find out who killed you. Your choice. Strip or I'll make sure there are only four of you Devils."

The idea of making him strip seemed ludicrous when it popped out of her mouth, but now her nipples pebbled with the idea of seeing Nate Marchand in the flesh. All the flesh. Her body pounded with anticipation and arousal. Nate looked murderous as he bent sideways to pick up the buttons she'd sliced off and put them in his pocket. The barrel of the gun slid against his skin, leaving a pink line on his throat.

When he started unbuttoning his shirt, she sat back and watched the show. The barrel of the pistol never wavered, but Elisa shook with the fierce need to touch all that she saw. Acres of maleness covered with a fine sprinkling of dark hair on his chest. Scars, too many to count, marred his skin.

After he removed his jacket and shirt, she swallowed hard.

"Now the pants and boots too." Her voice had become so husky, she almost didn't recognize it.

"What is the purpose of this?"

"I want to see you naked." It was the truth, at least part of it.

Apparently she'd shocked him though because his mouth dropped open and that's when she noticed the bulge. His trousers seemed to be much tighter than they had been earlier. In fact, he looked about ready to pop one of his own buttons.

"Let me see you." She stood and gestured at his remaining clothes. "I need to see you."

His gaze never left hers as he slowly removed his boots, socks and finally his trousers. He must have abandoned wearing drawers or he didn't have any left, because Nate Marchand was naked beneath the gray cloth. Amazingly, proudly naked with an erection that would rival a horse's.

He was blessed with a long, thick staff that jutted from a nest of dark curls, cupped by a pair of bollocks that made her fingers twitch to touch them. Her pussy throbbed with an awareness it had never before known. Elisa had images of her shedding her own clothes and lying down in the sweet grass with Nate.

"Now what?" he ground out, his gaze slipping to her shirt.

Elisa looked down, embarrassed to see that her very hard nipples were clearly visible through her homespun shirt. He already knew she wore no corset or female trappings, but now he knew that the sight of him naked made her body react.

"You can get naked too," he whispered.

Of its own volition, Elisa's hand put the knife back in the scabbard and reached out to touch him. Warm skin met sweaty palm and a jolt of pure passion raced through her. Her body vibrated with need, with want, with animal impulses that almost overtook her. Almost.

Instead, she trailed her hand down his stomach, touching each scar as she went, until she grasped his cock. It was as hard as a tree branch, and as hot as fire, her hand barely encircled its girth. He hissed in a breath and Elisa swam in the depths of heat she saw in his eyes.

"God has blessed you, Nathaniel Marchand. If we weren't enemies, I'd lie with you."

"I'm not your enemy."

"That's a load of shit, but I'll let it pass."

"So lie with me. I want you, sweet, beautiful Elisa." His voice, that honey-sweet voice, coated her, tempted her, called to her to do as he bade.

"I—I can't."

"Let me pleasure you. You can keep the gun if you'd like, but please"—he closed his eyes and sucked in a breath through his nose—"let me taste you."

Let me taste you.

Heaven help her. She'd never had a man say that to her before, or even had a man want to get in her britches before. Tragic thing was, she didn't know if he was lying or not.

"Why would you call me beautiful?"

"You are. Those eyes are as blue as the sky in December. Your skin is sweet as cream, and your breasts...ah, God, I'd give up a week of my life for one taste."

Nate knew how to seduce, that was for certain.

"How do I know you're not funning with me?"

He choked out a laugh and pressed her hand to his throbbing hardness. "Does this feel like I'm funning?"

No, it surely didn't. Elisa swayed for a moment, then threw her arms around his neck and pressed her body to his. The man was like an oven, heat radiated through him, bringing her to a boil. Her lips locked with his and she dove into a whirlpool of sensation.

Elisa let instinct guide her as mouths dipped and played. He cupped her ass and pulled her closer, nestling his staff against her pussy. Before she knew it, the bark of a tree was at her back and both her shirt and trousers were unbuttoned.

As his mouth continued to pleasure her, his fingers dipped into her honey and pleasure ricocheted through her.

"You're so wet, sweet Elisa," he whispered against her lips. "So wet."

She hoped that was good because she sure as hell felt good. He rubbed and circled the pleasure spot she'd discovered years ago. Only with him at the reins, it felt a hundred times better. Soon those questing fingers were sliding into her pussy even as his palm continued to rub her sweet spot.

"I need to get in there. Please, Elisa, let me in."

She nodded, lost in a sea of sensation and passion, eager to journey with Nate to wherever it would lead. His mouth found her nipples and she nearly cried out from the ecstasy. Somehow her trousers were down around her ankles and his cock had replaced his hand. Just as he slid into her, his teeth closed around her nipple.

Pleasure, pain and everything in between ripped through her as he impaled her, stealing innocence and gifting her with womanhood.

"Holy Christ." He cupped her jaw. "Why didn't you tell me?"

"Doesn't matter. Better you than some hairy, fat man Da picks out." She hadn't let loose the pistol and tapped him on the back with it. "Finish it, Marchand, and make it good."

He captured her mouth in a kiss as he slid from her body, only to fill her again. And so his rhythm was set, one designed to bring her slowly back to the brink of insanity.

"Faster." She bit his shoulder and rubbed her hardened nipples against the hair on his chest. Skitters ran down her body as he growled and captured the neglected nipple in his mouth and started fucking her in earnest.

Deep, slippery strokes pushed against her clit with each thrust. His roar of passion took her completely by surprise. She cried out a little, unable to speak, and her eyes closed with the spasms of her release. Nate bit her again as he found his own release, pulling her along on the road to heaven.

Their breathing was the only sound in the woods. The birds and insects had long since quieted against their passionate union. Elisa pushed against his shoulder and he stepped back, his cock sliding from her still hungry body. With a deep breath, she found courage she'd never known she had.

"Thanks, Marchand." She buttoned up her shirt and trousers with hands that surprisingly didn't shake. "I enjoyed that."

His eyes filled with fury. "I am covered with your virgin's blood and all you can say is 'Thanks, I enjoyed that'?"

He stepped toward her and she raised the pistol.

"What do you want me to say? Marry me, Nate?" She snorted. "That ain't never gonna happen, so I figured thanks would be good. It was definitely good, I'll give you that, but that doesn't change anything."

She circled around toward her escape, keeping her eyes on the seething, naked man in front of her.

"What do you mean, it doesn't change anything? It changes everything."

His dark gaze reflected confusion and anger. Elisa wouldn't fall for any of it. Her family was more important than anything she could ever have with a stranger who made her feel like a woman. A stranger who made her heart gallop and her body throb.

"No, you're wrong. You are still my enemy." Elisa ran, escaping the man who already owned a piece of her soul.

Chapter Five

Nate stood there trying desperately to catch his breath and locate his brain, which had relocated to somewhere between his legs. He couldn't quite bring himself to look at his dick or he'd see the proof of the innocence he'd just taken against a tree.

A tree!

God help him, his father would have whipped him with a switch, one of the thin ones that always stung the most. Gideon would likely tear his hide for this.

Nate wanted to redo the last thirty minutes. If only he'd told someone he was meeting Elisa. There went the "if only" problem again. He needed to forget about that and live with the regret now that he'd deflowered a young woman.

He smacked himself on the forehead and ran toward the stream. At least the temperature of the water would cool the boiling heat that still gripped him. He felt hunger for the voluptuous woman he'd had in his arms a few moments ago, a hunger that hadn't been satiated by one encounter. Even now, he hardened just thinking about her curves, her breasts and the sweetest pussy he'd ever had.

Without forethought, Nate brought his right hand to his mouth, the hand that had been pleasuring her, and sniffed. Her scent washed over him and damned if all the blood didn't pool in his nether regions again. Just to torture himself, he licked his finger and her taste coated his tongue.

"Shit, shit, shit." He jumped into the one foot deep stream and rubbed himself raw with the sand from the bottom, washing away any trace of Elisa Taggert from his skin.

Too bad he couldn't erase her from his memory. She'd taken up residence and it didn't seem likely she would leave anytime soon.

After drying himself off with his shirt, he dressed in his remaining clothes and went back to the camp. Gideon eyed his bare chest with raised brows, but said nothing. Zeke gestured for him to sit. Lee and Jake were nowhere to be found.

"Did the talking work?" Gideon asked.

Nate shook his head. "No, not a whit." Thank God Gideon didn't know exactly what had worked.

"I figured as much. I think we've got a plan." Gideon gestured to Zeke. "Listen to what he has to say."

Nate turned to Zeke, his stomach clenching at the thought of facing Elisa again.

"I've got Lee and Jake doing reconnaissance to verify my theory, but I think this will work." He drew a circle in the dirt with a stick. "Here's the Taggert ranch, approximately fifty acres. The cattle are here." A smaller circle within the first. "The house is here." A square within the larger circle. "The tree line is here." A bunch of squiggles above the square.

"That sounds correct from what I remember."

"Me too. Your Elisa surprised us from here."

As Zeke pointed at the squiggles with the stick, Nate's stomach tightened so hard, he thought he'd be sick.

Your Elisa.

"There must be a path from behind the house to the trees. Something hidden and known only to the Taggerts. If we find that path, we can surprise them and take either the old man or the boy." Zeke's brown gaze met Nate's. "Your Elisa then has no choice but to agree."

Your Elisa.

"Stop calling her that. She's not my Elisa, no matter what happened."

"What do you mean no matter what happened? I thought you said she only kissed you."

Damn Gideon and his perceptive mind. Nate searched for something intelligent to say.

"What I mean is, she's not, nor will ever be, my Elisa. Now let's focus on successfully completing this mission and not on the girl."

"Agreed. Now the key is going to be timing. I believe they take twelve hour shifts watching the herd. I doubt the old man gets on a horse anymore." Zeke squinted at the horizon. "If we surprise them halfway through a shift, one will be asleep and the other unsuspecting."

It sounded like a marvelous plan, one that was sure to work. So why did Nate feel like a snake in the grass? It was an honest job, one that had been verified on paper.

"Your Elisa is going to be a tough opponent to beat."

That did it. Nate's sleeping temper exploded.

"She's a stubborn, ill-tempered, illiterate girl without the sense God gave a goose. That combined with our purpose here and her personal hygiene habits are a sure bet that Elisa Taggert is not my kind of woman. I don't like her, nor will I ever like her. She's beneath me." Nate didn't mean a damn word of what he said but it all tumbled out of his mouth like a black cloud. "We'll do well to finish this job as quickly as possible and be away from Grayton, Texas."

A rustling was the only warning before a redheaded snarling beast exploded from the bushes, her pistol cocked and aimed at his head.

"You're a lousy excuse for a human being, Nathaniel Marchand. At least your friends have the courtesy to give me credit for being smart. You have no idea who I am or what I am, but you pass judgment like some preacher." Her eyes glittered dangerously. "I should put a hole in your head this second for what you said about me especially after your cock was just inside me not thirty minutes ago. You bastard."

She smacked him on the side of the head with the pistol and the ringing felt like his death knell. God knows he deserved it.

"You will not capture any of us, and you ain't gonna make us leave the land my grandfather owned. I am a part of this dirt under your feet and have more right to it than Samuel O'Shea ever will. He stole the land from my mother while my da was away at war. However he did it, she ended up dead by her own hand while he told everyone she wanted her children to be safe in his care."

She laughed, a choked, mournful sound that made the hairs on Nate's arms stand up.

"His care? The first thing he did was try to kidnap me. I've kept him off my land for more than a year. If you think you and your friends can succeed where he's failed, go ahead and try. I guarantee you that someone will be dead before it's over."

Elisa smacked him again, and he felt a trickle of blood by his ear. He took it like a man accepting punishment for his sins, without protest or denial. He dared not look at Gideon and see the condemnation in his eyes.

"Now you've got two choices, leave now or stay and be ready to go to war with the Taggerts." She stepped back toward the trees, her gun still rock solid in her hand and aimed at Nate's head. "If you were any kind of men you'd take the first choice."

"I'm sorry." He said it without thinking. His heart squeezed painfully around the vicious, cruel words he'd spouted about her.

Nate finally met her eyes and recoiled from the hurt and fury he saw in their blue depths.

"Too little, too late, Frenchie. I hate you."

She was gone without a whisper of sound. The far-off echo of hoofbeats was the only indication that she'd left entirely. Nate was afraid to move, to breathe, for fear the world would come crashing on his head.

"I'm not going to ask you anything, Nate, but I'm hoping you'll be kind enough to tell us what the hell just happened." Gideon's voice permeated Nate's pain-filled stupor.

Nate took a shallow breath and realized his entire body trembled. He held up two fingers, asking for a precious snippet of time to regain control of himself. He thought it would be a good job, a new start for the Devils. Instead he'd plunged himself into a hell of his own making.

"She's not like any other woman I've ever met."

"That's obvious. I've only seen you lose control once before, and I never expected it over a woman." Gideon knew him better than anyone.

"She's strong, aggressive, outspoken and...she makes me feel alive, for the first time in a long time." Nate knew Zeke and Gideon would both keep his confidence and he needed to tell someone how he felt. "I don't know what happened, but somehow I ended up with her in my arms and my head buried so far up my ass I couldn't even tell what day it was."

Gideon touched him on the shoulder. "She's a powerful woman to have that kind of affect on you. Are you committed to the Devils?"

"Yes, absolutely." There would never be a question of that.

"What about this job? It's not too late to tell O'Shea no." Gideon forced Nate to meet his gaze. "You're hurting, I can see that, but I need to know that you're with us on this job or we'll move on."

Nate couldn't possibly live with that. Turning down enough money to feed them for two years because he thought with his dick instead of his brain? It wouldn't, just couldn't, happen.

"We're going to finish this job, no matter what. I'll keep my distance from E-Elisa." Although he wasn't prone to affection, Nate gave Gideon a quick hug. "You are my family, and my loyalty is to the four of you. Always."

Gideon looked up at Zeke who nodded.

"We won't tell Jake and Lee about this, but we'll have to rethink our plan, especially considering she heard every word of it." Gideon shook his head. "She's going to give some husband a hell of a ride."

Nate swallowed hard. If circumstances had been different, he'd never have met Elisa Taggert. If circumstances had been better, he might be the one marrying her.

ဆုလဗ

Captain Nessman rode up to the general store with his grudge firmly stuck in his craw. Those damn rebel bastards.

They'd been telling the truth about working for O'Shea, but he'd been evasive as to what exactly they were doing for him.

Nessman dismounted from his Army issue horse and cursed the stupid nag. They paid for greenbroke wild horses and got the bottom of the barrel. Stupid thing constantly tried to bite him. Two ladies walking down the street eyed him with concern until he smiled and tipped his hat.

"Good morning, ladies."

They nodded and moved off, apparently unwilling to speak to an Army officer. Texas had, after all, fought for the Confederacy and resentment ran high and wide. He didn't give a shit though. His quarry was the Devils.

As soon as he stepped into the general store, he knew the owner was a man to be reasoned with. A mousy little man with beady eyes, he gave Nessman a toothy grin.

"G'mornin' to you, Captain."

"Same to you. Captain Elliot Nessman." He held out his hand and was rewarded with a clammy, limp hand in return. Nessman extricated his hand from the other man's grip quickly. "I was hoping you might be able to help me with something."

"Anything you need, sir. My name is Marvin Scofield and I own this establishment. I'd be happy to assist you." The little man definitely knew how to butter his bread.

Excellent news.

"There's a group of five men camped just outside town, apparently working for Mr. O'Shea."

"Oh, yes, I know one of them sir, a Mr. Marchand. I hung up his advertisement there." Marvin pointed to the window. "Mr. O'Shea hired them right quick."

"Do you know what for?"

"I think it was to get rid of the Taggerts." Marvin shook his head. "Sad story actually."

"And who might the Taggerts be?" He was so close to catching the Devils, closer than he'd been in months. Nessman could almost taste victory.

ಹಿCಚ

Elisa shook with rage and hurt. She'd never been on such a wild ride of emotions before. Damn Nate Marchand. Before he'd stepped into the store, her life had been hard, but bearable. Now it was on the verge of being hell on Earth.

She rode like she was being chased, more than likely by her own conscience. Elisa had been the instigator, as usual, the one who found trouble no matter where it hid. She'd wanted to humiliate him, to make him regret ever agreeing to work for Samuel O'Shea.

Instead, she'd fallen a little in love with him. He hadn't given an inch of his pride, standing there buck naked. Truth was, he probably could have disarmed her easily but he hadn't. She'd suspected he was a gentleman by the way he spoke and acted. However, the way he'd allowed her to hold her power had convinced her of that fact.

Then she'd gone and done it again. Stepped from the frying pan into the fire...into his arms. And Lordy it was hot, hotter than the flames of Hades. She'd been scorched by it. Her body felt sore and still sizzled from the memory of the heat. For some strange reason, she'd wanted more, more of the magic she'd felt in Nate's arms.

Now she knew it had been a sham—a way for Nate to take control over her physically without actually putting her in chains. He'd thought her beneath him. *Beneath!* Just because she wasn't book-learned or went to some fancy school didn't mean she was beneath anyone.

It hurt. It hurt bad. Enough to bring tears to her eyes, something she swore she wouldn't ever do again after her mother died. Now here she was practically blubbering over a man who took her virginity. At least now she was spoiled goods and maybe no man would come sniffing after her. That'd suit her just fine. She didn't need any man by her side.

Elisa was strong. She'd stand alone and protect her family and land. Nate Marchand had no idea what he'd thrown away, but she'd show him. She'd show him good.

The ride helped clear her head of the cobwebs of confusion that surrounded her. Nate and his friends were skilled, better than average, perhaps nearly unbeatable. Elisa would do her damnedest though. She rode out to Daniel, who looked about ready to fall asleep. It was no life for a fourteen-year-old boy, but he took the responsibility like a man.

Elisa was proud of him, although if she dared said that to him, he'd probably blush and tell her to go to hell. He was Irish, after all.

"What are you doing here?" he asked when she got closer.

"I need to talk to you." She reined up beside him and gazed over their precious herd. "Those five men O'Shea hired are plotting to kidnap you or Da to try to get me to give in. They already know a lot about us and what we've been doing so we need to change our ways for a bit."

He nodded. "I didn't get a good look at them, but they seemed pretty big. Who are they?"

"Ex-Johnny Rebs. I don't know from where, but likely Alabama or maybe Georgia. I'm guessing they worked together in the war."

"That'd make them pretty fierce then, since they survived." Daniel might be a boy but he was even smarter than Elisa.

"You're right. Since they survived together, they probably are very fierce. We're just going to have to outwit them." She reached over and grabbed his hand. "I need to know if you're ready to try. We can take what we have and leave Grayton."

If Daniel said he didn't want to fight, it would hurt, but Elisa would accept it. She didn't want to fight alone, and without her family, it wasn't worth the fight anyway.

"I don't want to give in to that bastard. Let's fight, Lissy."

He looked so grown up at that moment, Elisa's breath caught. She'd always thought of him as a boy, but she realized now that their life had turned him into a man early. Just as she'd grown into a woman too soon. Their childhoods had both been cut short.

If she had anything to say about it, their lives wouldn't be.

₧C&#x6;

The Devils finally agreed that a multi-pronged attack would work best. Since they outnumbered the Taggerts five to three, it would be easy to overwhelm them if the Devils each attacked from a different angle.

Attacked seemed like a strong word to Nate, but since it was a battle of wills, it was appropriate.

"What time will we do this?" Jake seemed so serious, so unlike himself. He must have sensed how grave the situation had become, even if he didn't know the details.

"Don't we want darkness to cover us?" Lee appeared calm, for once.

"No, not the dark," Nate offered. "We don't know our way around there well enough. The Taggerts grew up learning every nook and cranny of the land. We need to catch them by surprise."

"I agree." Gideon rolled a cigarette as he stared into the fire. "What about at dawn?"

"That's what I would do." Zeke snatched the cigarette from Gideon, then lit it with a burning stick from the flames. "They won't be expecting it so soon either."

"You mean tomorrow?" Nate shouldn't be surprised. They always acted quickly and decisively.

"Yes, tomorrow." Gideon put the stamp of approval on the plan, which meant it was now set in stone. "Ready to ride?"

Those three words had been said and responded to so many dark times during the war. It was a splash of cold water on a warm night, a shock to Nate's system.

One by one, they all responded, as they always had.

"Ready."

The rest of the night passed with everyone completing their preparatory tasks in silence. Nate had to stop himself more than once from telling Gideon that they shouldn't proceed with the job. Things hadn't gone too far yet, no blood had been shed.

Except Elisa's virginal blood. That was the reason he stopped himself from speaking out. His reasons had everything to do with his feelings about Elisa, and nothing to do with whether they could or should succeed. War wasn't about feelings, it was about victory.

An hour before sunrise, they rode together until two miles from the Taggert land, then split up as intended. Nate easily found his way through the half-light to the trees behind the house. He was to be the bait for Elisa while the others focused on Daniel and Sean. Guilt gnawed at him, feeding on the conscience that had reared its ugly head.

Patches of fog hung near the ground like a shroud. The humid air bathed his face, foretelling the heat of the day to come. A woodpecker tapped out a rhythm while the drone of a beehive buzzed in the distance. The sunrise couldn't be far off.

A mourning dove's coo—Gideon's signal to move—rang out in the early morning and Nate started toward his target. Bonne Chance picked his way across the forest floor, avoiding the stumps and fallen logs. There didn't appear to be any bogs or water, which was lucky. He constantly scanned all movement around him, waiting, expecting Elisa.

A rebel yell made Nate almost jump out of his saddle. Lee's voice carried for at least half a mile, and he wouldn't have let it loose unless he needed help. Nate kicked his horse into action and burst from the forest at a dead run. He released the snap on his holster, ready to pull his weapon if need be.

As he rounded the corner by the house, he saw shadows grappling in the field next to the barn. He headed straight for them, hoping he'd arrived in time. As Bonne Chance came to a halt, Nate jumped off the horse and threw himself forward, anxious to help Lee.

"No, you idiot! It's a trap," Lee snapped.

Too late. Nate stepped right into it and it closed up tight behind him. Three of them, Lee, Nate and Jake were tangled in rope netting covered with some kind of sticky substance. His feet and arms felt heavy, weighted down by whatever that stubborn little cuss had put on the ropes.

"What the hell did she do to us?" Lee punched out, clipping Nate on the jaw.

"Don't punch me, you idiot." Nate tried to fight back, but got tangled even further.

Jake grunted. "Whose bright idea was it to steal the horses?"

"Yours, fool," Lee groused. "Now we're caught in this shit and it's all your fault. Then hero-boy comes along and gets stuck too."

"Hey, I was trying to help." Nate sighed and realized the smell coming from the net was honey. Honey and something else, something rancid.

Gideon arrived within moments. "Stop struggling, all of you. Zeke is right behind me. No doubt we're not going to have a successful mission. What the hell is that smell?"

"Honey and horse shit," Jake grumbled. "And it's one hell of a trap."

"Hold on, I'll cut you out."

Gideon and Zeke spent several long, excruciating minutes cutting through the ropes. Jake was the first one free. He shook his head like a dog and then pulled his own knife out to assist. The sun peeked over the horizon, bathing them in a pink light.

Nate and Lee were freed within another five minutes. Each of them smelled and stuck to everything they touched. The honey had congealed and begun to crystallize in the warmth.

"I don't even want to get on my horse." Nate spit out a mouthful of honey.

"I don't think the horse would let you." Jake laughed. "You stink."

"I think Miss Taggert has proven that she's a worthy adversary." Gideon wiped his knife off on his pants and tucked it away in the scabbard. "How the hell did y'all get stuck in this thing anyway?"

Lee picked up a lump from the ground. "This is why." He tossed it toward Gideon. "It looked like a sleeping girl just waiting to be caught by us stealthy marauders."

"The nets had a tripping mechanism somewhere," Jake offered. "I felt it close around my ankle and then all hell broke loose. Lee tried to help and the second net closed on him, then Nate found the third one."

"Dammit, we've wasted another day." Nate punched the corral fence post. Frustration raced through him, or was it a guilty conscience in addition to humiliation? He'd been caught in a simple trap by a not-so-simple girl.

Elisa watched from the tree line with a grin on her face. She knew the stupid trick wouldn't work more than once, but it was fun to watch grown men get caught in it.

She cupped her hand and called, "You can come back for more any time you want."

A few curses and grumbles met her offer. They walked away shaking off the honey and Midnight's evening pile of shit. Next time, she knew they wouldn't be so unsuspecting.

Ten minutes passed before Daniel appeared behind the house with a smile and a wave. Elisa took her rifle and walked toward him, ready to start their day in earnest.

Chapter Six

It took more than hour to get the damn sticky stuff off. The stream wasn't deep enough so they followed it until they found a pond. Fortunately, Nate had purchased soap and the three of them could wash themselves and their clothes. Nate would never eat honey again. Cursed stuff was like glue. It would be molasses for him from now on.

Gideon was the only one left at the pond. Everyone else had gone back to camp, their moods ranging from annoyed, to amused, to downright furious.

Gideon, however, seemed thoughtful. "Your Elisa got the best of us today." He held up his hand. "Don't even bother telling me she's not *your* Elisa. I can see the truth in your eyes, Nate."

Nate slapped at the water, spraying the bank on the other side of the pond. "I never intended on anything happening between us. She's a girl, Gid." He met his friend's gaze. "And she was a virgin."

"That certainly complicates things."

"I know. Believe me, I know it." He swam toward the grass next to Gideon. "I have trouble accepting that it even happened. It was so fast, so surprising... I lost control."

Saying it out loud did not make him feel any better. If anything, it made Nate feel worse.

"We all lose control now and then. You're human." Gideon put a blade of grass between his thumbs and blew, a high-pitched whistle sounding from the vibration. "The question is, what do we do about it?"

"Nothing. We can't afford to turn down this job." Nate rubbed himself dry with his blanket then put on blessedly clean clothes that didn't smell of honey and horse shit.

Gideon grabbed his arm. "Someone's going to get hurt here, Nate, and it might be one of us or it could be one of the Taggerts."

"I am well aware of that fact." Nate hadn't slept because of it, amongst all the other things that had happened since he met Elisa.

"Can you live with that?"

"I have to."

"So be it."

⁞⁞

Rodrigo appeared at their camp during the dinner meal. They'd all been lost in their thoughts, eating the simple ham biscuits and brooding. No one stood to greet him.

"Rodrigo," Gideon said much more casually than Nate could have managed. "What brings you by?"

"Mr. O'Shea wanted to know what's been happening. We hear things." The dark-eyed man smiled at each of them. "A week has already gone by without word. Just wanted to see if you have any information."

Nate unlocked his tongue. "It hasn't quite been one week. Right now we're doing reconnaissance and determining the best method of removal."

"You do talk fancy, don't you?" Rodrigo laughed. "I don't know what half of what you said means." His charming persona was gone, in its place the gun-toting hired man who had lurked behind his eyes.

Nate had to force himself to hold back the anger. "I am educated, Mr. Rodrigo. I use my education to the best of my abilities. Now, was there something specific you needed to know?" His palms couldn't get any sweatier and Nate's left eye started twitching from all the tension and stress surrounding them.

"How long?"

"How long for what?"

"Don't play fucking games with me, fancy man." Rodrigo caressed the pistol riding his right hip. "How long until they are gone?"

"I can give you an estimate, but not an exact number." Nate wiped his mouth with the handkerchief that he'd carried for four years, one that was almost see-through from countless washings. It represented the last piece of civilization he'd kept from Georgia.

"That's not good enough." Rodrigo's gun started to clear leather, and before it could, four men were on their feet, guns in hand.

Nate continued on, as if his friends weren't facing down death in the form of an obnoxious lackey. "Please tell Mr. O'Shea that our estimate is two weeks to complete the job. If that changes we will be certain to let him know." He didn't know what kind of game O'Shea was playing, but he wasn't about to join in. They'd agreed on a month, and hardly any time had passed. Nate's instincts were screaming that something was wrong.

Rodrigo's lips compressed as he graced each of them with a death-wish stare. "I will tell him, but know this, if this takes more than two weeks, you will deal with me and my men."

"Duly noted. Thank you for coming by, Mr. Rodrigo." Nate's voice shook a little, his heart thumped so loud it echoed in his ears, but he didn't think Rodrigo noticed.

Walking backwards, Rodrigo returned to his horse and mounted. After one last demonic stare from the bowels of hell, he rode off into the afternoon sun. Everyone let out a breath and the tension eased a little.

"That one is as trustworthy as a weasel," Jake said as he plopped back on the log he'd been sitting on.

"A dangerous weasel." Gideon looked at the retreating back of the man called Rodrigo. "We'd best remember that he has no compunction about killing any of us." He turned to Nate. "Do you think it will take two weeks?"

"It had better not take any longer than that." Nate couldn't stop the feeling of dread that gripped him. O'Shea and his men were all dangerous. The Devils just needed to do the job and get out of Grayton as fast as possible before they fell into trouble they couldn't get out of.

୫୦୯୪

Over the last few days, the Devils had been gentle with the Taggerts, willing to try tactics that would guarantee no bloodshed. Unfortunately they'd run out of choices and it was time to use other, more aggressive means.

Jake wasn't happy about it, but he salted the well, then stood guard on the path leading to the stream to block their access to the water. Zeke and Lee set up a watch on the way into town. Gideon and Nate rode up to the front porch, expecting Elisa to shoot them.

"So you're back, are ya?" The old man sat out in front again, this time simply rocking and staring off into the distance. "I thought my Elisa run ya off."

"No, sir, she didn't run us off. We're here to rightfully assert Mr. O'Shea's claim to this land." Nate dismounted. An itch in the center of his back alerted him she had him in her rifle sights.

"Bah! O'Shea's an idiot and so are you if you think this land belongs to him. My wife's grandda settled this land and my grandchildren will run cattle on it." He turned surprisingly clear eyes to Nate. "You'd do best to leave now or I'll shoot you meself."

As far as Nate could tell, the old man didn't have a weapon, not even the whittling knife. Nate wasn't afraid of him, but he respected him.

"I understand you might be confused by all this, sir, but your wife—"

Sean moved so fast, Nate almost missed it. He ducked in time to avoid the first swing, but the second one caught him on the temple. Stars exploded behind his eyes and the ground threatened to meet his face.

He heard Gideon shout and a struggle ensued between the three of them. Sean seemed intent on pounding Nate with his remaining strength, while Gideon insisted on stopping him. Curses peppered the air and Nate grabbed Bonne Chance's reins to steady himself.

The old man got in a kidney punch and before Nate could stop himself, he responded. His fist slammed into a jaw and a rifle shot split the air. The gasp of pain he heard sounded like

Gid, but they were in a pig pile and he couldn't tell who was who.

"I've been shot," Sean cried out.

"Oh hell, so have I." Gideon groaned.

Nate got up on his knees and assessed their wounds. The bullet had passed through the fleshy part of Gideon's arm and then grazed the old man's shoulder.

"Jesus Christ, what happened?" Gideon ground out.

"I have no idea, but this old man is stronger than he looks." Nate glared at Elisa's father.

Sean punched him in the ear this time. "Don't you call me an old man."

The three men probably would have been locked in combat for God knows how long, but the sound of footsteps from behind made them all stop dead.

"Get offa him."

The young voice didn't belong to Elisa. Nate assumed it was her brother, Daniel.

"Son, your father's the one who started this."

"Don't call me son, you rotten bastard. Now get offa him. I ain't gonna give you much more time."

Somehow they untangled themselves and Nate was dismayed to see that Gideon's arm was covered in blood. The injury was much worse than he'd first thought.

"Can I at least see to my friend's wound? After all, it was probably your sister who shot him." Nate's temper flared. That particular fact angered him more than anything. She drew first blood and had put all their lives at risk by shooting.

"Elisa doesn't miss what she's shooting at." Daniel's voice was full of pride.

"This time, she also shot your father."

"You're a liar!"

"While she was busy trying to shoot Gideon, the bullet went through him and grazed your father's shoulder. Look, just look." Nate still couldn't believe she'd done it. It was very unlike her to be sloppy. Elisa was as precise as Nate was.

"Da? Are you hurt?" Daniel leaned over and peered at his father.

Sean got up on his hands and knees, his face gray in pallor. "I think I've been shot."

Daniel glared at Nate and Gideon. "Get off this land. Get off, get off, get off!" Passion and fury that would rival his sister's blazed from his young eyes. Telltale beads of sweat made their way down his baby-smooth cheeks. The boy didn't even shave yet and here he was holding a rifle on two men.

Nate helped Gideon to his feet. Keeping an eye on the boy, Nate took his neckerchief off and tied it around his friend's arm like a tourniquet. Gideon was a little pale and swayed just a bit on his feet. Nate wasn't sure if it was from losing blood or getting punched in the head by Sean. Nate's ears still rang from the old man's hard fists.

"I said, get off this land." Daniel waved his weapon around, poking his finger at Gideon's wounded shoulder.

That was the breaking point for Nate.

He stepped right up to the rifle and pushed the barrel into his stomach, daring the boy. Nate was so angry that Elisa had shot Gideon, he wasn't thinking clearly.

"Listen to me, boy. We were hired to remove squatters from land legally purchased by Mr. O'Shea. Your family has done nothing but fight us at every turn, and now you've shot one of us. What do you think that means to your chances of staying on this land?" Not that there was a chance they'd stay on the land, but he had to try to get one of the Taggerts to see reason. Perhaps it wasn't too late for the boy.

Daniel's eyes widened, but he kept a firm grip on the rifle. "I still got a bullet in here, mister."

"You'd better pay attention then. Your sister made a grave error in shooting Gideon. When she draws the blood of one Devil, she incurs the wrath of all of them. I won't forgive this and I sure as hell won't forget it."

Nate glanced at Gideon sitting on his horse, watching the byplay between Nate and the boy. Something like pride shone in his eyes. Gid had always been like an older brother to him, even though Nate had felt like an outsider, the only non-Blackwood in the Devils. Knowing that Gideon was proud of him gave Nate an extra measure of self-confidence. He poked his finger in the boy's bony shoulder.

"You tell Elisa that the Devils will be coming back and this time, there won't be any childish tricks. We will remove the Taggerts from this land."

Elisa watched Nate and his friend leave, one obviously injured. She'd been trying to scare them, not shoot them, but her hands shook on the rifle. Something that hadn't happened before. Although she hated everything Nate and his friends were doing, she was glad she hadn't killed them. Elisa hopped on Midnight and kneed him into motion. As they cleared the trees, she heard Daniel shouting her name.

"Elisa, come out please. I don't know what to do." He sounded like a little boy again, a boy in dire need of his big sister.

A surge of red-hot anger shot through her at the thought that Nate or his friend had hurt Da. She raced to the house with the wind at her back. When she reached the clearing, she slid off Midnight's back and hit the ground running. Da sat on the edge of the porch with blood dripping down his arm.

Elisa's heart almost stopped beating.

"Da!" She dropped to her knees in front of him, desperately searching for a wound. Dust and dirt coated his face, but the only blood was on his arm. Thank God.

"What happened?"

Daniel's eyes narrowed. "You shot him."

The words fell like a hammer on an anvil. "Wh-what?"

"You shot him when you were doing your fancy rifle trick for those men. Bullet went straight through that curly-haired fella and grazed Da." Disappointment reflected in his gaze. "How could you?"

"I shot him? Da, I shot you?" God help her, she'd made mistakes before, but none this big.

Until now.

"That you did, Elisa girl. Stings like a bitch too. Pardon me language." He groaned and clutched his shoulder. "Can one of ya get a bandage or somethin'?"

Elisa jumped up and ran for the well, eager to retrieve something to help her father. Her stomach rolled and her breakfast tried to make a reappearance. When she pulled the bucket back up from the well, the smell of salt water hit her nose.

Bastards!

They'd salted the damn well, those lousy snakes. Well, Da might not like it, but she'd have to use some whiskey to clean the wound instead. Later she'd go down to the stream and get some fresh water for them. She dashed into the house and took the whiskey bottle from behind the flour—whether or not he actually thought it was hidden was a joke between her and Daniel. On the way back out, she took a clean piece of linen from beside the sink.

"Oy, you're not using me whiskey, are ya?" he cried, eyeing the bottle in her hand with dismay.

"Da, we need to clean the wound and this is the only thing we've got." She sat next to him and poured some into the linen.

"What about water?"

She'd purposely sat on the side with the wound so he couldn't stop her from using the whiskey. She realized that he was talking and acting like his usual self. Perhaps the fight over the land had finally worked its way into his befuddled brain. Thank Holy Mary and all the saints.

"They salted the well. We'll need to go to the stream and there's no time. I need to take a look at you."

With a grimace, she ripped his shirt to get to the wound. Not only had she shot him, but she'd ruined one of the few good shirts he had left. She couldn't sew worth a damn, Mama had always done it. They didn't have the money to pay for anyone to sew so they'd made do the last year.

Now Da only had two shirts, and one of them had a missing sleeve with a bloody hole in it thanks to Elisa. The wound was superficial, but it had burrowed a gash about two inches long on his arm. Enough to sting and bleed a little. The bullet had been hot enough to nearly cauterize the skin so thankfully no stitches were needed.

With a lot of cursing and complaining, he made it through her nursing. When she tied the sleeve off as a bandage, he swayed against her.

"Why don't you go inside and lay down? Daniel needs to get back to the herd and I need to go get water."

"Yes, yes, that's a good idea. I'll just go lay down for a wee bit." He disappeared into the house without the old man shuffle she'd come to dread, a fact that Elisa did not miss.

"He acted almost normal." Daniel's comment echoed Elisa's thoughts.

"He's still in there, Daniel. We just need to bring him out." She glanced at her brother. "Hopefully before we're either killed or lose our land."

After Daniel left to go check on the herd, Elisa loaded up to go to the stream. Although they didn't normally keep a guard on the cattle at all times, she'd been worried Nate and his friends would hit when she was taking care of her father. He'd known Da had been wounded and any good soldier attacks when the enemy is weakest.

Suddenly everything overwhelmed her, and Elisa fell to her knees next to her horse. A great, gusting sob burst from her throat as grief, anger and frustration waged within her. Damn Samuel O'Shea and his black heart.

Damn Nate Marchand for making her fight a battle she didn't want to. In another time, she and Nate might have sparked. But now, all she could do was load her weapons and hunker down for a fight.

It took several minutes for the shakes to pass, then Elisa got to her feet, wiped her eyes and squared her shoulders. She had to be strong for her da, her brother and for herself.

Time to throw herself back into the fray and go on the hunt for water.

⁞⁝

Nate signaled for the others with his whippoorwill call and headed back to camp with Gideon. Nate helped him down from the horse, under protest, and sat him down by the dead coals of the fire. Within minutes, he had a fire going and water bubbling to clean the wound.

Lee and Zeke arrived and curses, along with appreciation for the fine shooting on Elisa's part, rained in the air. Zeke sat and assessed Gideon's wound.

"It's gonna need a stitch or two." He glanced up at Lee. "Bring me the pouch with the medical kit in it."

Lee did as he was bade without argument. If Gideon was in trouble, the Devils were as serious as a group of gravediggers. None of them could bear to think about Gideon *not* being part of them. Even though the wound wasn't life-threatening, the very sight of his blood brought home the reality that this job wasn't going to be easy.

"Why don't you go relieve Jake at the stream? He's always had a hand at stitching," Gideon said to Nate.

"Good idea. Besides he's been waiting out there for at least four hours. He probably needs a rest." Nate put his hand on Gideon's good shoulder. "I'm sorry you got shot."

"It's not a big deal. It was either me or you going to take that bullet. At least she's got good aim and didn't hit me any higher or lower."

"That's the gospel truth. I'll see if I can find us a rabbit or something for dinner too. You'll need some red meat." He nodded to Zeke and Lee, then mounted Bonne Chance.

The ride out to the stream was uneventful for the most part. The birds sang, the squirrels chattered and the bees buzzed. Life appeared to be normal for most of God's creatures. Too bad mankind couldn't get on that wagon too.

Nate still hadn't quite accepted that Elisa had shot Gideon. He held the realization back, keeping it at bay until he was ready for it. The ability to control his emotions wasn't easy, but he'd had plenty of practice. Being poor had taught him how to grin and bear hardship, his parents had taught him how to bury his feelings deep inside.

One night when Nate was eight, his mother simply walked out of their house and never returned. Nanette Marchand had apparently had enough of being a wife and mother, and chose not to stay any longer. Within a few months, he received a letter from her in Atlanta, telling him that she loved him but she just couldn't stay.

His father took the abandonment hard, as hard as Nate, but he drowned his sorrows in liquor. Too many times his father had come home barely able to stand, yet strong enough to whip Nate for his transgressions, real or imagined. Afterwards, Nate would clean up the blood and vomit and make sure his father slept comfortably. And so it went. By day, his father was a teacher, by night, a demon of enormous proportions to a young boy. He'd spent his childhood both hating and loving his father.

Until Nate met Gideon Blackwood and his life changed irrevocably. Accepted as a friend, Nate felt like he'd found the family he'd never had. The brothers and cousins didn't seem to care that Nate was the poor son of the town drunk. They spent their teenage years doing all the crazy, silly things young men do.

Then came the war and again, Nate's life changed. It seemed he was doomed to having the rug yanked from under him, so to speak. As soon as he was comfortable and felt even the tiniest bit secure in a situation, all hell broke loose.

Now he'd met Elisa Taggert and damned if it didn't feel like the rug had slipped again.

∞∞

Elisa heard men's voices as she approached the stream on foot. She'd tied Midnight to a tree and crept up to the water. It was a good thing too because someone else was already there waiting. She'd bet a nickel it was one of Nate's friends. They were exceedingly smart men who knew that once she discovered the well had been salted, she'd head for the nearest fresh water.

Two of them stood by the bank of the stream talking. One was a redheaded man with bright blue eyes, the other a brooding Nate. Her heart did a somersault and she silently cursed the wicked thing.

"Gideon's okay though, right?" the redhead asked.

"He'll be fine. Zeke's taking care of cleaning him up, but he thought you should be the one to do the stitching." Nate tied his horse off at the bank.

Elisa knew they were talking about the one who'd been shot, whose name she now knew was Gideon. She listened but her eyes kept straying to Nate's hands. The memory of them still haunted her dreams, awake or asleep.

Focus on what they're saying, you ninny.

"Never thought my mama being a seamstress would come back to bite me in the ass." The redhead chuckled as he swung up onto his horse, a nice-looking bay. "I'll send someone to relieve you in four hours."

After the other man left, Nate sighed long and hard, then leaned his head on the horse's neck. He spoke softly enough that Elisa couldn't hear what he said, but she recognized the posture—one of emotional overload. She understood it too well. The last three years had been a constant barrage of pain and suffering.

She had to convince Nate and his friends to leave them be. Shooting Gideon probably wouldn't help her in the long run since they were still standing guard over the fresh water supply. Elisa had to hold back a humph from escaping. Men could be the most perverse creatures on the planet. No doubt they considered it an insult to their honor and would want to avenge their friend.

Elisa had to stop that from happening, at any cost. A sudden thought struck her and it took her several minutes to work through it.

If she had time, she knew she could change Nate's mind...so she'd steal the time.

By kidnapping him.

Chapter Seven

Elisa slithered through the bushes, careful not to disturb even one branch. She knew the woods like the back of her hand and it served her well on more than one occasion. Like now. She picked up a tree branch just the right size for her hand from the ground nearby. Elisa hoped she wouldn't have to use it, but it was important to be prepared.

Nate appeared to be caught up in talking to his horse, giving Elisa even more opportunity to surprise him. She tried not to notice the way his trousers hugged his behind, or the way his shoulders filled out his jacket. She shook off the creeping heat that threatened to take over her body.

He cleared his throat and stepped away from the horse just as she reached him. The gun slid from the holster and she pressed it into his back, cocked and ready.

"Don't move."

His entire body stiffened. "What are you doing?" he snarled.

"I'm taking care of my family. You'd do best to remember that I'd do anything to protect them. Now, walk."

Nate didn't move, which didn't surprise her. Elisa nudged him in the back with the nose of the pistol.

"I said, move."

"I'm not going anywhere. You'll just have to shoot me because you're really good at that. You shot Gideon and you shot your father." His harsh words cut through her. Even if it was the truth, they hurt. Badly.

She didn't want to be reminded of the injury to her father, particularly since this man and his friends were the reason she'd been shooting in the first place.

"We're going to walk to the stream now and you're going to fill my waterskins." Elisa could get used to this ordering thing.

"Do it yourself. See if you can get past me."

He threw down the gauntlet and Elisa was never one to ignore a challenge.

"If that's what you want, Frenchie."

Dealing with rough cowboys came natural to her. She'd done it all her life. When her father was away in the war, she was the one who ran the ranch, not her mother. Her mother didn't want or know how to deal with everyday details a ranch required.

At the age of fifteen, Elisa had already been ordering men around. Ordering this one around wouldn't be a chore. It would be a pleasure.

"Walk."

"Make me."

Elisa backed up a step. "You sure you want this, because when I give it, it's going to be everything. I'm not gonna hold back for you."

He snorted. "You may not be an itty-bitty thing, Miss Taggert, but I outweigh you and I'm stronger than you. I'll bet you I'm also angrier than you. You shot my best friend. What makes you think that I will simply do what you tell me to do?"

Nate started to turn and Elisa knew she only had seconds to grab control of the situation before he overpowered her. In less than a second, she put the gun back in its holster and had the tree branch firmly gripped in both hands. With a mighty swing, she hit the back of his knees.

He shouted and fell to the ground, bracing himself with his hands. Elisa paused, holding the tree branch above his head, blocking out the memory of just how soft those brown locks were.

Her heart thundered and her blood whistled through her veins. She hadn't felt this alive in years. "I've got plenty. Do you want more?"

"Give me all you've got," he taunted.

"You've got it." She didn't want to kill him, but she sure as hell wanted to disable him.

He grabbed her ankle and flipped her on her back. Before he could do any more, she scrambled away, keeping the branch in her hand. Nate was quick though, he had her other ankle in hand and yanked. Within seconds, Elisa was again beneath his hard body staring up into his furious dark eyes.

"You make me lose control." He said each word deliberately. "I can't believe you would shoot at us."

"You're trying to take everything from me. What would you do?"

For a moment, just a brief moment, his anger faltered and confusion moved through his eyes. With her left hand, she took hold of the back of his neck and pulled him down, slamming his lips onto hers. She kissed with all the pent-up anger, frustration and lust brewing inside her. His lips were as hard as granite, but his body couldn't lie. She felt his cock lengthening against her and a pulse echoed through her body—of need, of desire, of all that she couldn't have, shouldn't have.

Elisa swam in a sea of arousal, floating on the tingles that raced through her. She knew she should stop kissing him, but he began to kiss her back after several beats. Languorous heat shimmied down her skin from the contact. Nate damn sure knew how to kiss. Reluctantly, Elisa pulled her mouth away and bit him on the lip.

Before he could recover from the kiss or the bite, using all the force she could muster, Elisa swung the branch with her right hand and conked him on the head. His breath gusted past her lips and he was still. His heart beat against her chest so she knew he lived. She hoped like hell he wasn't playing possum.

"Nate?" She wiggled beneath him. "Nate?"

He didn't answer. Now all she needed to do was figure out how to get a two hundred pound man off her. Without Nate holding up his weight, she found it hard to breathe.

It didn't matter how she did it, Elisa would get him to her house and convince him to leave Grayton. This was her opportunity to make him see what she needed him to so he would know what O'Shea had done to her and her family.

ഇരു

After the third time Elisa failed to hoist him up over the horse, she stopped to take a break. She knew she took a chance, but danged if she didn't need some water. After quickly filling her two waterskins, she rushed back to Nate. He still lay unconscious, his hands and feet secured by the rope she'd found on his saddle.

His saddle! That was it. She could use it as leverage to pull him up onto the horse. Elisa set the waterskins on the ground and ran over to him. She picked up the rope and dragged him fifteen feet until he lay next to the horse. The leaves in his hair would be the least of his worries when he woke up.

After making sure the beast was calm and secured to the tree, she looped the rope around the saddle. The horse shied a bit when she tugged the rope taut, but she turned and started pulling with all her strength. Slowly but surely Nate's arms came up, then his shoulders, soon, she could see the top of his head above the saddle.

The man must have weighed eight hundred pounds, not two hundred. Her boots dug into the soft ground as she tugged and yanked, and the rope nearly cut a rift in her shoulder. By the time he was belly down over the saddle, she shook from the effort and sweated buckets beneath her shirt and hat. Nate groaned and Elisa jumped a foot off the ground, her heart lodged in her throat.

Time to go.

Nate came awake slowly, the rhythm he felt beneath him was Bonne Chance, but he wasn't riding the horse. He was laying belly-down on the horse. Not exactly dignified.

That's when he realized his hands were tied, and if he wasn't mistaken, there were also ropes around his waist and feet. He was tied to the saddle.

Elisa.

The last thing he remembered was Elisa. She'd caught him unawares in the forest near the stream. He'd been angry, furious really at the little girl who shot Gideon. When she'd appeared, it was almost as if he conjured her from the depths of his anger. She'd tried to force him to do something...get water, maybe?

It was all a little blurry, but he distinctly remembered her hitting him in the back of the knees with something. More than likely, a piece of wood, and then...she'd been under him. Again. The sweet softness of her body was like heaven and hell. He remembered a kiss, a bite and then nothing after that.

Elisa must have hit him over the head, probably with the same damn stick she'd used to smack him to his knees. He begrudgingly gave her credit for taking him down. How the hell she got him on the saddle, he had no idea, however his arms felt like they'd been ripped out of their sockets so he could guess.

It appeared that he'd underestimated Elisa Taggert again, something he was getting very good at. He heard a second horse and figured it was her. If he played his cards right, he might be able to take her by surprise. He didn't know what he could do with his hands and feet tied, but Nate would not go down without a fight.

They stopped ten minutes after Nate woke. He blocked out the pain and discomfort, a trick that had come in handy many times in the past several years. It was the only way to maintain control. He heard the creak of leather, then her boots hit the ground when she dismounted. Staying still was difficult, but he kept his eyes closed and strained to hear every sound.

She walked away from the horses, and all was silent. Nate counted to sixty, slowly. Then counted again. When she didn't come back, he opened one eye and looked straight into Elisa's amused blue eyes. She leaned against the side of her house, arms crossed, with an annoying smirk on her face. Nate's anger surged anew.

"I had a feeling you were playing possum."

"Untie me and let me go."

"What makes you think I'm going to do that?" She pushed off the wall. "Embarrassed, Frenchie, that I got the better of you?"

"No." A lie, of course. "So far everything you've done can be excused under the law as protecting your property. When you kidnapped me, that crossed the line into unlawful. Any judge in this state would put you in jail for what you just did. We weren't even on your land."

She shrugged. "You're probably right. It doesn't matter because it was worth it."

"At least let me get off the horse." He didn't want to admit it to her, but riding like that had made him sick to his stomach. Nate certainly didn't want to vomit in front of her. She more than likely thought he was an incompetent man already. No need to add fuel to the fire.

"Okay, I'll get you down. It might not be pretty, but I'll get you down."

"Just do it." He gritted his teeth, figuring the only way she could get him off was to either push him or pull him. That meant he was either going to land on his head or his ass.

"Don't try anything funny." She plucked a rather nice knife from her boot. Coming up behind him, she untied the rope around his waist. "Now I'm going to push your shoulders. I'm afraid you're going to land on your ah, behind."

"That's fine, just get me off of here."

"Don't say I didn't warn you." Elisa took one of the ropes off his ankles, then came around to the other side.

When she stepped in front of him to undo the loop from his wrists, his knuckles brushed against the front of her trousers. It was as if he'd been struck by lightning. It appeared that anger and passion were intertwined between them. Wherever Elisa Taggert was concerned, Nate was helpless to control his body's reactions.

She sucked in a breath and moved back several inches. That let him know she was just as affected as he was.

100

Information he could use to get himself free. Nate was on his own to escape. No doubt the rest of the Devils wouldn't even know he was missing for hours.

"Are you ready?"

Images of Elisa beneath him and on top of him assaulted him. Lord, help him, he was obsessed. For a moment, Nate couldn't remember what she was asking him, or why. His mind had been caught up in the possibilities of being intimate with Elisa again.

"Ah, yeah, I'm ready."

"You can push yourself backwards when I push at your shoulders. One, two, three!"

The combined forces of both of them moved Nate only six inches. His chest compressed on the top of the saddle.

"Go, go, more," he gasped out.

She ran around to the other side of the saddle, took hold of his waist and pulled. This time he found himself back to belly on top of her. Not exactly the position he wanted to be in, but at least he was off the damn horse. He took in a deep breath.

"If you're through, roll to the left or the right," she snapped.

Nate waited another couple beats before he moved, just to remind her that although she had him tied, he was still bigger, stronger and dangerous. The battle raged on.

Elisa didn't know what to do with him so she brought him in the house and stuck him in her bedroom. Then, in a twist of perverse satisfaction, tied him to her bed. He almost didn't comply, but when she stuck a gun in his face, he must've remembered what she was capable of.

After she finally got Nate settled, she was able to check on Da. She took one of the waterskins from the table where she'd left them. Da sat in his usual rocking chair on the porch, staring off into something only he could see.

"Da?"

He continued to stare. When Elisa handed him the water, the makeshift bandage on his arm was a painful reminder of what she'd done earlier.

"Drink something, please."

"Already had me some whiskey. I don't need anything else." He sighed. "Your ma would've been proud of you."

Elisa's heart clenched so fast and hard, it hurt all the way down to her toes. He didn't talk much about her mother, and when he did it was usually to tell Elisa to hush up. She'd always wondered how her mother had felt about her, if she'd considered Elisa a worthy daughter. Elisa had spent so much of her time on the back of a horse, in trousers, getting dirty, shouting and working so hard she nearly passed out each day. Not very feminine at all.

Her mother had never told her she was proud of her. To hear her father say it so matter-of-factly took Elisa by surprise.

"Do you think so?" She was glad her voice didn't shake or betray the power his words had.

"I do. She wasn't as strong as you, Elisa girl. You have the strength of Irish queens running through ya. Pride, temper and red hair. You're Irish through and through. Your ma, bless her soul, was half-English. She just didn't have it in her to be so strong." A lone tear skidded down his wrinkled cheek. "I never said it before, but you did good while I was gone. Taking care of things. I'm only half a man now, but you and Daniel...you make your da proud, too."

The lump in Elisa's throat grew to enormous proportions until she finally swallowed it. "Thank you," she whispered.

"What are you going to do with that fella in your room?"

"You saw that?"

"It was hard not to. I was sitting at the table when ya stumbled in pointing a gun at him. Did ya not see me?" A wisp of humor colored his words.

"No, I didn't." Dammit, she'd been so focused on Nate, the entire group of his friends could've been there and she'd have missed them too.

"No matter. I was keeping watch for ya." He finally turned to look at her and Elisa was pleased to see the spark of life in his eyes. A spark that hadn't been there in over a year. "You be careful. I see things and that man is dangerous."

"I can handle him, Da. He's tied up."

Her father shook his head. "That's not what I meant. You guard your heart from him."

Elisa almost told her father it was too late. Her heart had already been captured by the ex-Confederate soldier with the soulful dark eyes and the fancy words.

"I'll be careful. I promise."

After her conversation with her father, she sat at the kitchen table, head in hands, trying to conjure a plan of action. How exactly was she going to convince this angry man, a man she'd been intimate with, to tell O'Shea to go to hell?

Elisa had no choice but to reveal everything to Nate and hope he believed her.

Nate stewed in angry silence. No matter how hard he wiggled, pulled or yanked, the ropes binding him to the hellion's bed weren't budging. It had only been a short time since she'd left him, but it felt like days. He couldn't even swat the fly that had landed on his nose.

He might be helpless, but the situation wasn't hopeless. He had a plan for the next time she untied him, which would be soon, or he'd soil her linens.

With nothing but time, he examined the room. It contained a bed, a stool, a small table with basin and pitcher and hooks on the wall. There weren't even any dresses hanging on the hooks, just trousers and shirts that could belong to a man. It was neat and tidy with very little to indicate that a woman lived there. The only feminine touch was a silver-backed hairbrush on the windowsill.

It appeared out of place in such a Spartan room. Elisa did have incredibly lush hair. He expected she'd need to brush it frequently or risk it turning into a snarled rat's nest. A few auburn strands hung down from the side of the brush, taunting him. It was definitely *her* brush. A reminder that beneath the rough exterior lay the heart and body of a woman.

A woman who was driving him insane.

The door opened and she walked in, a small book and papers clutched in her hand. He sensed nothing from her but determination—she didn't even look concerned that she held a man hostage on her bed. Nate had to admire her gumption, at least a smidge anyway.

"Are you here to untie me?"

"No."

Not one to mince words, was she?

"Why not?"

Elisa took the stool, brought it next to the bed then sat. "I need to tell you a story."

"Although I'm in your bed," he growled, "I don't want to hear a bedtime story. I just want to leave. Now."

"You're not leaving until you hear me out, so you might as well quit your whining and listen." The stubborn jut to her chin punctuated her words.

Of course, he should have expected that condition. "Start talking quickly then or I'm going to soil your bed."

"Should I get you a pot?"

Oh the indignity of even contemplating that. Nate couldn't, wouldn't ever piss in a pot in front of a woman. The very idea made his balls crawl up an inch or two.

"No thank you. I don't believe I will use a chamber pot with you holding my, ah, instrument." Heat seeped into his cheeks and he was thankful for his natural tan skin tone.

"Instrument?" She laughed, a husky chuckle that echoed across his skin.

"I was raised a gentleman, Miss Taggert. I treat ladies, women, with respect." He sounded haughty even to his own ears.

"Hm, okay, I guess I dropped down a notch from lady to woman." She waved the papers. "It doesn't matter. Just let me know if you're going to bust."

"Most assuredly." Nate was already planning an escape. He would wait for the right moment to do so, then Elisa was in for a surprise of her own.

She opened the book and tucked the papers beneath it. "This is my mother's journal. Take a look at her penmanship." Leaning over, she held the book up for his inspection.

Nate noted flowery, neat script that was most definitely a woman's. He couldn't quite read the words, and she pulled the book away when he tried to.

Elisa tucked it beneath the stool and stared at the papers for a moment. Nate couldn't help but notice it was not her usual behavior, and that intrigued him, more than he'd admit.

"This here is the bill of sale for the property signed by my mother and"—she cleared her throat—"the note that says she took her own life. In it, she said for O'Shea to look after us instead of my da. It just didn't make any sense."

Nate's anger dissipated. He'd had no idea that her mother had killed herself. His attention was riveted on the evident grief shadowing Elisa's beautiful face.

"She, ah, had a hard time when Da went away to war. He waited two years to volunteer, and when he left, she fell to pieces. Sat in her rocking chair by the window, staring into nothingness." She glanced up at him. "Sounds familiar, doesn't it? Da sits in that same chair now, like a ghost for her ghost."

Nate couldn't stop the questions from rolling around in his brain and one popped out before he could snatch it back. "Who ran the ranch while he was gone then?"

"I did." Her blue eyes burned with remembered pain.

"How old are you?"

"Eighteen, but I'll be nineteen in three weeks." She shrugged. "We do what we have to, otherwise life ain't worth two bits."

Her words rang with truth. He'd spent many hours agonizing over choices that he had to make in order to live. Although Elisa hadn't been in the war, she'd been a soldier anyway. Nate did some quick math in his head.

"So you were fifteen when you took over this ranch?" Impossible.

"Sounds about right. We had a foreman and a half dozen ranch hands on the Circle G. Within a couple of months after

Da left, O'Shea drove or scared the cowboys away, and bought the foreman, Rodrigo, off." She looked down at the papers still clutched in her hand. "Daniel was eleven. I had to be strong for him so I fought back. Most folks might have rolled over and played dead, but I had pride, dammit."

Nate snorted. "I'd say you have that in abundance, as well as intelligence, quick wit and stubbornness."

She frowned at him. "I'm not sure if you just insulted me or not."

"Take it as you will." He tried to see what was written on the papers. "So your mother sold the ranch while your father was off to war. Why would she do that?"

"No, she didn't!" The vehemence in Elisa's voice echoed in the small room. "This isn't her handwriting and she damn sure didn't kill herself. Mama was a devout Catholic and never in a million years would she commit a cardinal sin like that."

She shoved the papers in his face. "Look at that handwriting. Just look. Is that the same handwriting in the journal? No, it's not. It's a man's writing. It's that bastard O'Shea's writing. What kind of idiot sells two hundred head of cattle and a ranch for twenty dollars?"

"Twenty dollars?"

"Yes, ridiculous, isn't it? Enough to feed us for about three months, if we eat bread and crackers." She shook with fury. "Then that son of a bitch strung her up from the rafters and left her for me to find."

Nate's heart ached for what young Elisa had seen. He was assaulted by a flash of the agony he'd felt upon discovering his father's grim corpse. This situation was much more than he'd anticipated. Now that he'd gotten close to Elisa, and knew her story, he no longer believed that money would solve the Devils' problems. He'd suspected this woman had power over him, now he knew for certain.

"Can you even understand what that feels like?" Elisa closed her eyes and took a deep breath.

"Yes, I can."

Her eyes popped open and she scrutinized his face. "I think you mean that."

"The handwriting on the note? Is it hers?"

"No." It came out in a rush that sounded like a sigh. "It was left on the kitchen table underneath the sugar bowl. The bill of sale didn't show up until five days later. They're both written in the same handwriting."

She held them up so he could see them. Nate took his time examining both documents and concluded that Elisa was telling the truth, if indeed this was the bill of sale and a suicide note.

"May I see the journal again?"

She hesitated. "As long as you don't read too much of it. Mama was...well, different than me. A dreamer. A lot of what she wrote was stories."

Elisa retrieved the book from beneath the stool and held it up. Nate was surprised to notice that her hands trembled. He would never have thought she would outwardly show any kind of weakness. After reading a few lines of something about a starry sky, he glanced back at the letters.

There was no doubt in his mind they were written by different people. If that were true, then O'Shea committed murder and fraud. Nate's innate sense of justice reared its head and poked at his heart.

"Elisa, I..."

She threw the papers on the floor and stood, staring down at him. Her hands reached for the buttons on her shirt. He couldn't help but gape, caught like a deer in a hunter's sights.

"What?"

"I, uh, think you're right. These were written by different people." He swallowed as the second button popped free and a slice of peach skin appeared.

"So what are you going to do about it? Will you tell O'Shea you can't do the job?"

When the fourth button released, Nate's body pulsed with need. His cock grew to painful proportions at the sight of the shadows cupping Elisa's unbound breasts.

"I, uh, have to verify the documentation." Nate gulped. "I should be able to do that in the county seat."

She stopped unbuttoning and his entire body screamed in protest. "What do you mean verify?"

"I mean that you are a very smart adversary, Elisa. I have to verify that what you've shown me is the true bill of sale." It would also be wise to compare it to the one O'Shea showed him if he could. "It should be on file in the county seat. If they indeed match, then I can better present your case to my friends and we will decide together what to do." He needed to wipe the sweat off his forehead, but he was still tied to the damn bed.

"Do you do everything together?" She finished unbuttoning her shirt and without taking it off, untied the rope around her waist and slid her trousers off.

Nate was pleased to notice she only wore cotton drawers, ones that had seen better days, the holes making them that much more enticing. His mouth watered at the glimpse of inner thigh and the outline of her pussy.

"Yes, w-we, uh, became very close during the war. Each one of us complements the others, making us a whole." His fingers opened and closed, eager to touch and caress her skin.

"If you verify what I've told you is true, will you and your friends help me?" She climbed onto the bed, the shirt gaping open to reveal her beautiful breasts, the nipples begging to be pleasured.

"Yes, we'll help you. I promise." He yanked at the ropes. "Now untie me so I can touch you."

Elisa's mouth kicked up into a small grin. "Untie you? Now why would I do that? I think I like you at my mercy."

"Then have some mercy and let me taste you." Nate couldn't believe he begged, but when a man was desperate, he'd do what he needed to.

"Say please."

It was a battle of wills. Unfortunately his will was listening to his dick and it wanted Elisa.

"Please." He whispered it against her lips as her mouth descended on his.

Her agile fingers unbuttoned his shirt and trousers while her tongue danced and dueled with his. Raw heat ripped through him when her bare nipples touched his chest.

"You're killing me."

She chuckled with a hint of evil. "No, but I love torturing you."

Nate believed it. One hundred percent. For a woman who'd just lost her virginity, she was certainly skilled at seducing a man. Or perhaps it was just that easy to seduce him. He'd like to think it was the former.

Elisa pulled his trousers down to his ankles, effectively trapping him with his clothing and the ropes she'd secured him with. It bothered the hell out of him, but he was so far into the deep lake that was Elisa it was either sink or swim. He chose to swim.

"Are you going to do more than torture me?" Nate gasped.

"I wasn't planning on it."

Nate groaned from somewhere near his toes. "You're a witch."

Elisa raised one eyebrow. "You sure do know how to flatter a girl."

"I'm cocked and ready to fire, Elisa. If you don't want to be my target, then take your nearly naked body off me." There was only so much Nate could take, gentleman or no.

She must have seen something in his eyes because she removed her shirt and climbed off the bed to shed her drawers. Elisa stood there deliciously naked, with enough to keep him wanting for days, weeks or even years.

"What do I do?" she asked uncertainly.

Again, she reminded him that she was unskilled at things between a man and woman. Nate was struck with a moment of pride that he was the one she chose to gift with her virginity. The gravity of that fact had not escaped him.

"You ride a horse like you were born on one. Climb on and ride me, sweet Elisa."

Her gaze wandered to the hardened staff between his legs that jerked and begged for her attention.

"Please."

Elisa climbed on top of him and pressed her hot body to his. Her breasts pillowed against his chest with diamond-hard nipples scraping against him. Nate's skin sighed in pleasure. It felt like heaven had just landed on him.

"You feel hard." She wiggled a bit.

Nate groaned. "You feel hot."

"Mmm, so do you. What's next?" She pushed herself up with her hands so her breasts were inches from his mouth.

Nate lifted his head, but he couldn't quite reach them. She followed his gaze and, with a grin, leaned forward just enough that he could lick the raspberry peaks.

Soft, sweet, delicious. He lapped like a puppy at her nipples. Elisa pressed her nest of curls into his pulsing arousal and he thrust up against her. She gasped and did it again.

"If you bring these a little closer, I can do more than lick them."

Elisa nodded and inched forward. His mouth closed around the nipple at the same time the head of his cock nestled against her cleft. Moisture teased him as he sucked and bit at her.

"Oh God, that feels so good," she breathed.

Nate was desperate to touch her soft skin, to cup her ass as he slid into her.

"Untie me, sweetheart."

"Uhm, then we have to move."

"I promise it will be even better." He thrust upwards, rubbing her clit until she shuddered with need. "Come on, let me free."

Elisa sat up to straddle him, and when the full heat of her pussy encased him, he forgot to breathe. Sweet Jesus, she was perfect. He slid back and forth, absorbing the heat, the sensation, the pleasure.

After she freed his left hand, Nate grabbed one plump breast and held it to his mouth, sucking her deep while he continued to slide against her wetness.

When his right hand was free, he reached down to position his cock at her entrance. He couldn't wait any longer or his body would explode too soon without even being inside her.

"Now what?"

"Now you ride, sweetheart. Hang on."

Tight, so tight. Her pussy gripped him as he entered her inch by inch. It was only her second time and he didn't want to simply thrust in for fear of hurting her. He needn't have worried. She sat up and the movement pushed him fully inside her.

"Nate," she cried. "Oh my God."

The sheer perfection of the moment gave him pause. Nate had never experienced a flood of ecstasy so poignant, it made his eyes sting with moisture. It was as if they had been made to fit together.

He kicked off his pants and she groaned.

"Ready?" he said through clenched teeth.

"If I get any more ready, I'll be done." Her eyes were wide with arousal.

Nate strangled out a chuckle, hanging on to his own self-control with iron will. He cupped her round behind and pulled her up to the point where he almost slid out, then lowered her back down.

Elisa was a quick study. "I've got it now, cowboy."

She picked up the rhythm and rode him like any good horsewoman. A slow canter designed to drive him mad.

"Can we pick it up to a trot, at least?"

"Hmm, how about we just head for a gallop?" She leaned down and fused her mouth with his, tongues tangling briefly.

When she sat up, Nate decided he'd never seen anything so beautiful. Her unbound, riotous hair, the sheen of perspiration on her freckled face, the pert nipples tight enough to cut glass, and the expression of pure pleasure. He drank it in like a thirsty man, eager to quench his need.

He reached up and tweaked her nipples while she showed him exactly how she could gallop. Fast and fierce. Her pupils dilated until he saw almost all black and he could tell she was close. He held back, pulsing with the need to spill his seed. Nate was still a gentleman and wanted to be sure Elisa found her own release.

One hand found her hot button and rubbed it between thumb and finger. Within moments, she clenched around him so hard, he saw stars.

"Nate!"

His orgasm ripped through him making lights sparkle behind his eyes and his heart thump so hard, he thought it might crack a rib. He thrust upwards, burying himself deeply inside her, so deep he knew he touched her womb, her soul.

Nate's fingers dug into her hips as hers dug into his shoulders. After a perfect, amazing minute, the waves of ecstasy began to recede. She collapsed on his chest, breathing hard from her gallop.

"Holy shit."

Nate chuckled. "I wouldn't quite put it that way, but I agree with the sentiment."

She pinched his arm. "You talk too fancy."

"My mother insisted on it." He kissed her forehead. "It's a habit now."

When she slid off him, his body cried out from the loss of her heat. She snuggled up next to him and laid her head on his shoulder.

"That was even better than the first time."

He wrapped her in his arms and they lay together as man and woman. The tremors of their lovemaking still shook his body.

"If I hadn't seen it myself, I wouldn't believe it. You are a natural temptress, Elisa Taggert." He pressed his lips to her temple.

"You'll do as you promised?" She twisted to look up at him, her eyes once again crowded with shadows.

"Yes, I will, but no more shooting or fighting."

"Can we do this again?" One of her fingers twirled the hair around his nipples.

"I don't think so."

"Why not?"

Nate didn't know how to explain to her that he had no intention of marrying her and therefore couldn't imagine taking advantage of her again. At least that's what his brain said.

"I'm not staying in Grayton after this is all over."

She frowned. "I know that. I'm not asking you to marry me, Frenchie. I liked what we did and I want to do it again. Where's the harm?"

"The harm is in the fact that we're not married and this could result in a child. Are you prepared for that?" He didn't want to be so blunt, but in the ways of the world Elisa was still so young.

She scoffed. "I can't catch a baby that fast. Besides, it doesn't matter. Any child that I bear will always be loved."

It was that simple to her, but Nate knew better. There were worse things in the world than having a bastard child, but he didn't want her to have to bear that burden because he couldn't keep his pants buttoned. Regardless of what Elisa wanted, Nate would not make love to her again.

Chapter Eight

Nate waited until she slept before he left her bed. Drained emotionally and physically, he could barely think past the fact that he needed to get away from Elisa. At least for a little while. He'd promised her he'd look into the bill of sale and he meant it.

He'd be walking a fine line between his loyalty to his friends and his need to fulfill a promise. Bonne Chance was tied to a hitching post in front of the house. Elisa's father was nowhere to be seen, thank God. Nate hopped on the horse and rode like the hounds of hell were nipping at his heels.

When he reached the camp and came tearing in like a madman, Zeke and Lee jumped to their feet, guns at the ready.

"What's wrong? Why aren't you at the stream?" Zeke glanced at Gideon sleeping comfortably under the trees.

"Where's Jake?"

"He went to town to get some medical supplies. We used up all the bandages on Gid." Zeke grabbed hold of Bonne Chance's reins. "Now, tell me what's wrong."

"Elisa Taggert kidnapped me." He spit the words out of his mouth like a bad taste.

"What? What did fancy pants just say?" Lee hooted. "Oh, how the mighty have fallen."

Nate didn't respond to Lee's teasing, he met Zeke's concerned gaze. "I need to talk to Gideon."

"I think you're right." Zeke's careful expression revealed nothing of what he was thinking.

Nate hoped his actions didn't ruin his friendship with the only family he had. He walked over to Gideon, trying to determine exactly what he was going to say. Words had always been his shield against chaos, something he desperately needed now.

Gideon sat up against a tree, a bandage firmly tied around his left arm. As Nate approached, his eyes opened and he blinked a few times. His face was a little pale, but his eyes were as sharp as ever.

"What's happened, Nate?"

Nate sat on the grass beside Gideon and rested his elbows on his knees. "Are you feeling better?"

"It'll take a few days to get most of my strength back, but it's just an ache now. The bullet passed clean through the muscle, fortunately no bone damage."

Nodding, Nate chose his words carefully. "I've done something stupid, Gid."

"Tell me what happened. Something's been bothering you for days and you haven't said anything about it." Gideon was always the keenest of the bunch.

"I met Elisa Taggert the day we came to Grayton. Right then, I knew she was trouble in trousers. I tried to avoid her, but somehow we kept running into each other." Nate swallowed the regret he didn't have the right to express. "A few nights ago, after she caught me at the river alone, she forced me to take my clothes off and somehow we ended up having sex."

"Somehow?" Gideon raised one brow.

"Okay, it was the usual way only it was against a tree. My point is that I didn't mean for it to happen since she was a virgin." That fact still pinched his conscience hard. If he had known...that was just a load of shit. Elisa was in his blood from the second he'd seen her. Their joining was inevitable, and unavoidable.

"You took her virginity against a *tree*?" Gideon punched the ground. "What the hell were you thinking?"

"I wasn't thinking at all. Can you understand that? She makes me lose the one thing that makes me sane. I've lost my mind over her, Gid. I-I can't go two minutes without thinking about her." Nate's eyes stung and his heart wept with possibilities that would probably never happen. She'd never be his wife, never bear his children. The first woman he truly loved. After what he and the Devils had done or would do for the almighty dollar, he knew he couldn't ever be with her.

"I'm sorry, Nate."

"So am I, more than you ever know." Nate sucked in a much-needed breath and took a moment to regain his self-control. "There's more."

"I figured as much." Gideon gestured to proceed. "Go on. Let's hear all of it."

"She kidnapped me earlier today."

Nate didn't expect Gideon to laugh, but damned if he didn't burst out with gut-busting guffaws.

"It's not funny."

"Oh yes, it is! Nathaniel Marchand, the dapper, self-controlled gentleman, kidnapped by a young girl half his size." Gideon wiped his eyes. "It's more than funny, it's just deserts."

"I don't think it's funny. She practically took my arms out of my sockets and shaved a few layers of skin with that rope." Nate sounded petulant to his own ears.

"How did she kidnap you?"

"I don't want to tell you."

Gideon laughed harder. "Did she kiss you then knock you out?"

It was too close to the truth and Nate felt his cheeks heat. Gideon hooted.

"That's neither here nor there. After she got me back to her house, she tied me, ah, to the furniture and made me look at some documents. About O'Shea and her mother's suicide."

Gideon's laughter disappeared. "Her mother committed suicide?"

"Not according to Elisa. In fact, her mother's journal has different handwriting than the suicide note, and from the bill of sale supposedly signed by her. The really odd thing is the ranch and cattle sold for twenty dollars."

The truth was there in front of them. O'Shea cheated the Taggerts and murdered Elisa's mother.

"Do you have proof?"

"Not yet, but I have the bill of sale that Elisa claims is the real one. If I go to the local attorney who registered the sale and the county seat, I can compare this document to what's on file." Nate shook his head. "If it's true, then we're working for a murderer, trying to complete the destruction of the family he's already decimated."

He gazed into his friend's concerned blue eyes. "I don't want to do anything that will go against the Devils, but I can't, in good conscience, not investigate Elisa's claims."

"I understand." Gideon sat up straighter and stared into Nate's eyes. "Do you love her?"

Nate searched his heart and found a deep affection for Elisa that he'd never experienced before. That damn uncontrollable passion that made him think sideways. "I think I do. Gideon, what does that mean?"

"That means the Devils may have to switch sides."

Nate was afraid of that, afraid of what his carelessness might cost them, afraid his world had just fallen completely off its axis and headed out into the unknown.

"That might put all of us in danger."

"We've been in worse situations." Gideon sounded so matter-of-fact about it.

"Gideon, I don't want to risk your lives because of something I've gotten myself into." Nate's heart nearly stopped beating at the thought that his own stupidity might lead to the ultimate sacrifice by a friend.

Gideon touched Nate's shoulder. "There is nothing I wouldn't do for you, or for any of the Devils. You are my family, my brothers. We stand together as one, always."

Nate's throat closed up at Gideon's words. It was how he felt, but hearing it out loud was what he needed to grab hold of his runaway panic. They would stand together and fight together, no matter what side they were on.

"Do you understand?" Gideon's gaze never wavered from his.

"Yes, I do. Thank you, Gid." Nate shook Gideon's hand. "I couldn't, I mean, you all are..." Words failed him. Nate searched for them, but couldn't find what he needed. Elisa had turned him into a blithering idiot. An idiot who had to stop thinking with his dick and start thinking with his brain again. All their lives depended on it.

හ⊘හ

Jake Sheridan got by in life by being charming or sneaky depending on the situation. The curmudgeon who ran the general store wanted to know what the bandages were for, and when Jake wouldn't reveal the exact reason, the other man kept at it like a damn woodpecker.

"You're them fellas camped out on O'Shea's land right?" The older man grinned and Jake had to control the urge to roll his eyes.

"Yes, sir, we are. Doing just a spot of work for Mr. O'Shea." Jake glanced around the store. "This is a mighty fine store you've got here."

Marvin puffed out his scrawny chest. "Thank ya kindly. What did you say your name was?"

"Sheridan. Corporal Jacob Sheridan. A Confederate criminal."

Captain Nessman's voice crawled up Jake's spine. He had hoped to avoid seeing the man again, yet here he was like a boogeyman come to life.

"I am an ex-Confederate soldier, Captain Nessman," Jake said affably. "I'm no criminal."

A white lie, sort of. He hadn't committed any crimes in the state of Texas anyway.

"Was this man purchasing merchandise in your store, Marvin?"

The way he said the storekeeper's name made Jake's blood run cold. Something was brewing, which meant he was in danger. He had to get out of there fast.

"Thank you for your time, sir. I'll be on my way."

"No, he didn't buy a thing. Kept pestering me for bandages and such." Marvin sounded smug. "I think he might've stuck something in his pocket. Is he really a criminal?"

"Oh yes, he sure is. I'd be happy to take him into custody."

Before Jake could reach the door, Captain Nessman took him down with one punch to his lower back. Jake fell to his knees, trying to block the agony out long enough to get back to his feet and run. Pain exploded on the back of his head and the dirty wooden floor rushed up at him.

ෙ৪০৫৪

Elisa felt like grease on a hot pan, bubbling, jumping and popping. She'd had no experience being intimate with a man before. She couldn't help but think that perhaps telling Nate about Mama's death and the sale of the ranch could backfire and make matters worse instead of better.

After she cleaned up, it was time to relieve Daniel on watch. First she had to check on Da and make sure he drank some water. When she went into his room, the bed was mussed as if he'd been sleeping, but he wasn't there.

She headed into the kitchen and found coffee on the stove. Pouring herself a mug, she thanked whoever had been kind enough to make it. She hoped it would revive her, help her focus. It wasn't like her to be so confused and out of sorts.

"Do you love him?"

Da's voice from behind made Elisa jump a foot in the air and splash hot coffee on her hand. She yelped like an old hound dog. "Da, you scared me to death. What are you doing? Shouldn't you be in bed?"

"I'm sitting here drinking coffee. You came in, you paid me no never mind, figured you'd just wanted to get your own before you started talking." He sat at the table, a few crackers in front of him and a mug of coffee.

For the first time since Mama's death, Da seemed to be himself. He actually looked clear-eyed. Not only that, he looked like himself again. The little girl inside her wanted to squeal and run to hug and kiss him. It had been more than three years since any affection had passed between them. The very thought of following through on her impulse made her uncomfortable. It would be too awkward.

"I noticed you didn't answer the question, Elisa girl. Do you love him?"

She opened and closed her mouth without answering. She hadn't had a discussion with herself yet about how she felt about Nate Marchand. She had given herself to him, gifted him with the one possession a young woman could offer any man, ruined herself for any kind of proper marriage. Da's question was a good one, but it didn't have a simple answer.

"I'm not sure, Da. I...there's definitely something between us."

His bushy eyebrows rose an inch. "Something, eh? Sounded like more than something to me. You forget my bedroom is on the other side of the wall from yours."

Elisa's entire body flushed. She just knew her cheeks were like pink flags of naughty behavior. To think that Da had heard everything they'd said and done was more than embarrassing, it was mortifying.

"That's not what I meant." Elisa's natural defensiveness took hold. "Taking a man to your bed doesn't mean you love him, Da. Even women have needs."

"Needs, is it? I'd hoped we'd brought you up better than that. Your mother, God rest her soul, taught you how to be a lady even if you don't wear dresses. I didn't think you would have... Tell me this. Was this the first man that you were with?" Da's bald-faced questions made her squirm.

Elisa swallowed the denial that rose to her lips. He knew all about it. He'd heard it. No wonder he was sitting in the kitchen. Probably too embarrassed to sit and listen any further. Had she shouted Nate's name? She couldn't remember.

"Yes, Da, he was."

"That answers my original question then."

Was it that simple? Would she have given herself to anyone other than Nate? Did she love Nate?

"Da, I'm not sure that I—"

"I am. You've known love all your life, Elisa girl. You know I loved your mother, God rest her soul, more than life itself. And even though she wasn't as strong as you, your mother gave you and Daniel all the love she had."

She agreed with everything he said. Elisa may have grown up without a silver spoon in her mouth, but she grew up with something even more valuable. A family who loved her and each other.

"So I'm going to ask you one more time." Da leaned forward, his gaze intense and focused on her. "Do you love him?"

"Yes," she whispered, unable or unwilling to say it louder.

"Is he a good man?"

Elisa wanted to say no, but it wasn't true. Nate was a good man. "Yes, Da. He's an honorable man, and a good man."

"Will he help us?"

Anger with a healthy dose of frustration surged through her. Elisa threw the cup into the sink, coffee splattering all over the window behind it. "You've been sitting on that rocking chair for a year, letting me and Daniel take care of this ranch. Do you even know what's going on? Do you care? Suddenly you're here again and you want to know if a stranger can help us. A stranger who was hired to get us off the Taggert ranch. Where the hell have you been?"

Da responded with only one word. "Lost."

Elisa's tirade ran itself out and the hurt in her father's eyes gave her pause. She'd never been one to mince words, always called a spade a spade, yet this time she'd done some damage. The urge overcame her and she ran to her father. As she dropped to her knees, she wrapped her arms around his waist and tears stung her eyes.

He held her tight and whispered, "Elisa girl."

She finally had her father back.

༺ఌఄ

Nate readied Bonne Chance for the ride into town and then to the county seat, a city about thirty-five miles east. It would take him the better part of two days to get there and back, without running his horse into the ground. He wanted to be sure he was prepared for all eventualities, even those that required a gun.

As he tucked the hardtack and jerky into his saddlebags, Zeke approached him with worry in his normally blank expression.

"Jake's not back yet." Those four words dropped like chips of stone from Zeke's mouth.

"When was he due?" Nate didn't think things could get any worse, but perhaps he'd been wrong. Again.

Zeke looked off toward town, shading his eyes from the afternoon sun. "Almost two hours ago. He left right after he got back from relieving you. Something about stretching his legs and he offered to pick up some extra bandages."

"Did he specifically say when he'd be back?"

Zeke frowned. "No, but he's not one to be gone so long without word."

That was true. Jake might be a sometime thief, but he was a reliable thief who had spent the last fifteen years with the Devils. They all knew each other's habits inside and out. If Jake was late, then something was wrong.

"Gideon said you're headed out for a couple of days, taking care of the Taggert business." Zeke tucked his hands in his pockets.

"I was planning on it, but if Jake's in trouble then I need to stay."

Zeke held up one hand. "No, we need to figure out the Taggert situation. Lee can stay here with Gid while I go find Jake." He turned his brown eyes on Nate. "Be careful."

It wasn't said lightly. If anything, it sounded like a warning.

"You do the same."

"Come back as quick as you can. We'll just keep watch on the Taggerts 'til we hear from you." Zeke shook his hand. "She won't shoot us, will she?"

A grin crept over Nate's mouth. "I don't think so. She knows what I'm doing and why. We should have at least one day without any bullets flying from Elisa."

What he didn't say was that he couldn't guarantee the bullets wouldn't be flying from somewhere else.

"Rider," Lee called.

"Is it Jake?" Zeke asked.

"No, wrong horse and seat. I'd say it's that son of a bitch, Rodrigo." Lee sounded annoyed enough to shoot the man for even daring to approach their camp again.

Rodrigo.

Something Elisa said clicked in Nate's mind. She'd said their foreman Rodrigo had left the ranch high and dry. *Rodrigo.* What were the odds it was a different man? Not likely. That meant he had intimate knowledge of the Taggerts ranch—no wonder O'Shea had been able to perpetrate such crimes. Of course, Nate was assuming Elisa had been telling the truth about everything.

Nate ran over to Gideon, who had risen and started walking the fifteen feet to the camp. He strode as if he'd hadn't been shot six hours earlier. Nate shook his head. His friends were amazing men.

"I see him," Gideon said as Nate approached.

"I just remembered something. Rodrigo used to work for the Taggerts."

Gideon's head whipped around to stare at the approaching rider. "Unfortunate for them. What did he do?"

"Foreman."

"Ah, that's where O'Shea got his information."

Nate made a face. "No doubt. I don't want him to know about Jake missing or about me chasing that bill of sale. We need to keep him away from my horse."

"No problem. Lee can be his usual charming self." Gideon flashed a wolfish grin.

When Rodrigo arrived, he didn't bother dismounting, instead he stared down at the four of them. "Where's your friend?"

"Busy." Zeke's curt reply could have cut granite.

"Mr. O'Shea wants to know what's happening with the Taggerts."

"Plenty." Gideon's equally short reply echoed Zeke's.

"You boys can deal with me or you can deal with a posse of O'Shea's hands. Your choice." Rodrigo sounded as if he wanted to bring the posse back just to kick the shit out of the Devils.

Nate stepped forward. "Our original agreement was one month. We stepped up the timeline and told you two weeks, which was only three days ago. I don't know what the hell's going on, but rest assured, you can tell him that we are actively pursuing the rightful property situation of the Taggert ranch. I guarantee it."

His heart pounded at the thought that this man, this evil-looking piece of shit had been around Elisa as a young woman. No doubt he'd treated her badly and likely did all he could to destroy the Taggerts. The thought made Nate see red. Damn emotions kept getting in the way.

"Are we to expect visits from you every three days? If so, we can be sure to have tea and biscuits ready." Lee snickered.

"I can kill you where you stand, put you out of your misery since you're only half a man anyway."

Lee surged forward, but his brother stopped him inches away from Rodrigo. Zeke held on with enough force to make the veins in his neck stand out. Lee might only have one arm, but he had the strength of a bull.

"Tell Mr. O'Shea we send our regards." Nate gestured to the field behind Rodrigo. "I suggest you leave now before our half a man rips your head clean off your body."

With one last malevolent look at Lee, Rodrigo turned his horse around to leave. "I give you three more days and then you can answer to Mr. O'Shea himself."

"We look forward to it." Nate had trouble keeping the polite, stupid expression on his face. He didn't want Rodrigo to know how much it bothered him to have to deal with such a man, or to know that he had dealt with Elisa daily. Made his skin crawl.

When Rodrigo was just a spot on the horizon, Gideon turned to Nate. "Go now. See that attorney in town then head for the county seat. Lee, you stay here with me. Zeke, go find out what happened to Jake, quietly and without any fuss."

As they had countless times, the Devils took their orders and executed them without question. The tide had begun to turn and it appeared as though the Devils first business venture would fail.

Nate only hoped they'd all be alive after it was over.

∞CB

Nate found the attorney's office easily. It was the nicest house in town, a white clapboard with his shingle hung outside. The property was surrounded by beautiful trees and a perfect picket fence.

Obviously Alvin Potter was successful at the lawyering business. Nate didn't know what to expect so he had to be prepared for any eventuality. That meant he had to be ready to be friendly, formal or threatening.

Nate dismounted and secured Bonne Chance to the fence. After a deep, calming breath, he ran his hands down his trousers and jacket, smoothing any noticeable wrinkles and removing any debris and dirt that had settled on the fabric. He ran his fingers through his hair and straightened his lapels and collar. Since he was forever cursed with five o'clock shadow, he had shaved before setting off. His jaw was as slick as any professional attorney.

Nestled deep within his jacket pocket was the copy of the bill of sale that Elisa entrusted to him. He had to keep it safe no matter what the cost.

As Nate stepped through the gate, he heard a small dog barking and a man's stern voice. He couldn't quite decipher the words but the tone told him a lot. It told him that the owner of that voice expected things to be done precisely. That was at least a small amount of preparation Nate could carry with him.

The front porch was well-swept and well-kept, indicating a tidy man lived there. He rapped on the door three times and stepped back, his hands in front of him in a gesture of patience—something he was sorely lacking. Out of the corner of his eye, he saw Zeke riding down the street. Nate knew whatever had happened to Jake, Zeke would take care of it. That didn't make it any easier to ignore his fellow Devil if he needed assistance.

The door swung open and Nate inclined his head to the man who had answered the door. He was a rotund man of middle years with a balding head and half-spectacles perched on the end of his nose. He wore a starched white shirt with a blue vest, a gold watch gleaming from its small pocket. His round belly was covered with pressed blue trousers and shoes so shiny they could double as a mirror.

Nate drank it all in, assessing the best way to speak to Mr. Potter. "Good afternoon, sir."

Mr. Potter frowned, his eyebrows making a frightening, bushy V on his forehead. "Afternoon, stranger. What business do you have here?"

"My name is Nathaniel Marchand, Mr. Potter. I am in the employ of Mr. Samuel O'Shea to take care of some business with the former Taggert property. I had hoped, sir, that I could have your assistance in locating the bill of sale to prove Mr. O'Shea's ownership." Nate kept his voice crisp, businesslike, yet always polite.

"You're working for O'Shea then?"

"Yes, sir, I am."

Mr. Potter's rheumy brown gaze glanced up and down Nate's attire several times before he opened the door to allow him access. "I'm in the middle of something so we'll need to make it quick."

"Yes, of course, I understand and I apologize for intruding." Like hell. "I would have requested an appointment, but time is of the essence for Mr. O'Shea. He has asked my associates and me to resolve the matter post-haste."

"Yes, yes, of course, come in."

Nate stepped into a perfectly maintained house with gleaming wood furniture and not a speck of dust in sight. Potter ushered him into what appeared to be his office before Nate could get any more information to bring back to the Devils. The office was as neat as the rest of the house. Stacks of paper in regimented order, a bookcase precisely arranged, beautiful

Persian carpet and an enormous desk that must have been made from two entire trees.

"Well, you need a copy of the bill of sale for the Taggert ranch then?"

"Yes, sir, that would be extremely helpful."

Potter eyed him again. "What did you say your name was?"

"Nathaniel Marchand, sir, of D.H. Enterprises."

Potter's expression didn't waver from suspicious. "Now I can show you the bill of sale, but I can't make a copy of it for you. You'll have to go to Bellridge, the county seat, for that. You understand that, don't you?"

"Yes, sir. I had planned on traveling there for that very purpose, but I wanted to check in with you first to see if there were any additional papers that might be associated with the sale of the Taggert ranch." Nate hoped like hell he was making sense because he felt like a fly butting its head against a gas lantern, trying desperately not to get burned.

"Now I can't show you any other information, Mr. Marchand." When he pronounced the name incorrectly, Nate decided it was intentional. Mr. Potter liked to make people uncomfortable, probably gave him a sense of power.

Mr. Potter rose and went to the cabinet in the corner of the office. "Sit down now, this will take me a minute or two. The sale happened a year ago or so."

"I understand that, sir. I also understand that the Taggerts have been somewhat, ah, difficult in accepting the sale since it was the unfortunate Mrs. Taggert who sold the ranch."

"Ah yes, Melissa Taggert, a beautiful woman. Too good for the likes of that mick, Taggert."

Nate wondered if Mr. O'Shea knew how his attorney referred to Irish people. He doubted it.

After rifling through some papers with his chubby fingers, Potter came up with a piece of paper from deep within the cabinet.

"Here it is. Now as I said you may look at it, but you'll need to go to Bellridge if you want an official copy. We did give one to the family, but that wild girl is bound to have lost it. She's headed for eternal damnation, mark my words, doesn't listen to anything folks say. Wearing trousers and working and living all day long with men. Ruined for any kind of marriage and now this difficult situation with Mr. O'Shea." He tut-tutted. "That girl is dancing with the devil, she is."

Nate's hands fisted in his lap, but he didn't really care if Potter could see them or not. The fact that the man talked about Elisa as if she was a wild whore made the hackles on Nate's neck snap to attention. He knew firsthand that Elisa had been as pure as any virgin until Nate had made her otherwise, which still pricked his conscience.

Potter came back with a paper and eased himself into a beautiful leather chair behind the enormous desk. He read through the document two times while Nate sat there pretending to be patient, pretending not to want to punch the shit out of Potter.

Finally after what seemed like an hour, Potter held the single piece of paper out for Nate's inspection. "This is the correct document. You may read it."

"Thank you kindly, Mr. Potter. I do appreciate your assistance immensely." While his stomach threatened to return his breakfast, Nate concentrated on reading the bill of sale in his hand. He scanned the contents and, unsurprising, the paper matched that which Elisa had given him. The signature was not a woman's.

What Nate needed was to find any other documentation from the Taggert ranch that might have Melissa's signature on it to compare it to the bill of sale. If he didn't find anything in the hall of records in Bellridge, he might just have to ask Jake to do a little midnight visit.

With a smile that made his face hurt, Nate handed the paper back. "Thank you so much, Mr. Potter. Again I apologize for the intrusion. I just wanted to make sure I had the correct information."

"You're quite welcome there, Mr. Mar-chand. What is it that you and your associates, what was the name?"

"D.H. Enterprises."

"What is it that you do for Mr. O'Shea?"

Nate stood to leave. "Anything he needs us to." With one last nauseating thank you, he escaped Mr. Potter's office and house. Bonne Chance waited at the fence, ready for the long ride to Bellridge.

His mind whirled with the information he'd received. If anything, the visit with Potter confirmed that something was definitely wrong with the sale of the Taggert ranch. Generally wives were not allowed to sell property without their husband's signature. It's possible that Sean Taggert was presumed dead, killed during the war, when she sold the ranch. It was also possible that the laws in Texas were different. However, Nate knew something was wrong. He intended to uncover the truth and not just for Elisa, for himself. The Devils would make sure that the truth was served along with the justice.

Chapter Nine

Zeke rode down the main street in Grayton as if he hadn't a care in the world. He smiled, nodded and tipped his hat, while inside all he could think about was where was Jake? He thought about going to the general store since that's where Jake had been headed, however he also remembered Nate's warning about the owner of the store being a bit squirrelly.

If anything happened, it probably happened at the store or a saloon, the two places Jake had said he planned to visit. Zeke decided to start at the saloon, and it wasn't just because he needed a shot of whiskey, which he did. It was mainly because when men had been drinking, they were more likely to be talkative. Even some of the serving girls in the saloon were good sources of information. Zeke had a lot of practice listening.

Folks tended to fill in the silence since Zeke didn't talk very much, and when they filled in the silence, they filled in the details. There were two saloons in town. Not surprising. Although Grayton was one step above tiny, certainly with the number of cattle ranches in the area, there were a lot of cowboys who needed someplace to drink, let loose and have fun.

He chose the nastier of the saloons because Jake would have. He felt more comfortable amongst outlaws and thieves since he was a thief. A good one, but still a thief. As Zeke secured his horse to the hitching post, he heard the tinkling of glasses and some low conversation inside. The Blue Bonnet saloon across the street had no horses in front. This one, the Stone's Throw, had at least half a dozen. Definitely the better choice.

Zeke walked in and made a beeline for the bar. The air smelled of cheap whiskey, cigars and sweat.

The huge bartender had to be at least six and a half feet tall with shoulders and arms that had seen plenty of hard work. He had bushy hair and mustache and assessing blue eyes.

"Afternoon," Zeke said as he propped an elbow on the scarred wooden bar. "It's been a helluva day. I needed to wet my whistle and have myself some good booze."

"Then you're in the wrong place." The bartender guffawed at his own funny.

Zeke smiled. "I reckon that's true. How about you just give me a shot of whatever you've got? I ain't picky." He slapped down four bits.

The bartender poured him a shot in a questionably clean glass. Good thing Nate wasn't here, he probably wouldn't be able to drink from it. Nate was mighty particular about being clean. Zeke had seen Nate in front of the fancy white house and figured he was looking into the business with the Taggerts.

Gideon didn't give Zeke all the details, but he knew if anyone could find the truth, it was Nate.

The bartender decided to be chatty. "Just passing through?"

"Nah, just have a job hereabouts for Mr. O'Shea."

The bartender's eyebrows went up. "And you're drinking in here?"

Zeke grinned tightly. "I didn't say I worked for him. I said I had a job for him."

"Name's Clem," the bartender offered.

"Zeke."

They shook hands and Zeke knew he'd been absolutely correct about the bartender's strength. The man was enormous with a bone-crushing grip.

"I'm looking for someone."

The bartender gestured to the two women standing at the end of the bar, scantily clad, who were talking together. They wore clownish pancake makeup with bodies to keep a man occupied for hours, and no doubt Zeke would enjoy every second with them. Dammit. Right now his first concern was finding Jake.

Zeke shook his head. "Nah, I'm looking for my partner. Redheaded fella, tall, kinda thin, wears a flat-brimmed black hat."

"Doesn't sound familiar." Clem frowned. "I just got here. Sarah here was tending bar around noontime. She might have seen your partner."

"Thank you kindly." Zeke shot the whiskey down his throat. The slow burn took the edge off the anger and frustration bubbling inside him. He set the glass down and sauntered over to the two women.

"Which one of you is Sarah?"

The blonde with frizzy corkscrew curls sticking out every which way and the best pair of tits he'd seen in years, frowned at him. "That's not the way a true southern gentleman greets a lady. If you were a gentleman, you'd greet me properly."

The sweet sound of a woman with a Georgia drawl caressed his ears. This time Zeke's smile was genuine.

"Why, I beg your pardon, ma'am. Good afternoon, ladies." He took off his hat and did a short bow. "It's a pleasure to make your acquaintance. My name is Zeke Blackwood. How are you this afternoon?"

The dark-haired one tittered like an idiot and wandered away. The blonde one, he assumed was Sarah, sketched a small curtsey.

"Good afternoon to you, Mr. Blackwood. The pleasure is all mine."

"What's a Georgia peach like you doing in Texas?"

Shadows passed through her eyes. "I'd venture to guess the same as you."

Zeke understood. The war had been hard on everyone. They all did what they had to do in order to survive.

"Clem tells me"—he jerked his thumb toward the bartender—"that you were tending bar around dinner. I'm looking for my partner. His name is Jake. He's a tall redhead with an easy smile."

Sarah grinned. "I remember him. Sweet, charming. Nearly made this old whore blush."

"That's him." He could practically taste the information.

"He came after dinner at Arnie's and had a couple of whiskeys. We talked for a bit. He told me he had to go buy some supplies."

Zeke sensed there was more to Sarah's story. "Where is he?" It wasn't his way to be anything but blunt particularly when a friend's life could be in danger.

"I hear tell there's an Army captain in town, a Yankee."

Zeke's gut rolled at the thought of Jake in Nessman's hands. They'd been there and lived, but he didn't know if they'd survive again. Especially since Jake was alone.

"Do tell." Zeke slid a dollar bill under his hand on the bar to her.

She eyed it. "Word is that Marvin caught your friend stealing at the store and that Yankee captain put him in the jail. Said that he was part of a gang that had been bamboozling folks, possibly rustling." Her blue gaze probed his. "You part of that gang?"

Zeke swallowed the howl that threatened to escape. "There is no gang." He contemplated how much to tell Sarah. Since she was a fellow ex-Georgia resident, he felt he could trust her.

"That Yankee has been dogging us for months. He's looking, inventing reasons to put us behind bars. We're the only prisoners who escaped his camp during the war. He'd do anything to get us back under his thumb." Zeke shook with rage even thinking about Nessman.

Sarah nodded. "I was thinking it was something like that. I saw him down at Arnie's yesterday, gave me the creepy crawlies. You'll find your friend in the jail down the street. If you'd like, I can introduce you to Sheriff Turner. He's, ah, a friend."

"That would be much appreciated, Miss Sarah."

She inclined her head. "My pleasure, Mr. Blackwood."

Within ten minutes, Zeke and Sarah stood outside the stone jail. She pulled at the bodice that cupped her generous tits, then gave him a raised brow for looking. Zeke held up his hands.

"Hey I'm just appreciating the view."

"Hmph," she snorted. "Now, Jimmy is getting a bit long in the tooth but he's still up for a little flirting now and then. You let me get him distracted and then you can get your friend out."

As she opened the door, Zeke put his hand on her arm. "Why are you doing this?"

Her guarded expression became fierce. "I'm sick and damn tired of people like that captain taking advantage of folks just because they fought on the losing side of the war. That Yankee is an example of men who should never be given a sword to wield. Besides, your friend was cute."

Zeke didn't know whether to be appreciative of the support or stung by the compliment to Jake. Well, she hadn't mentioned him. He knew his blond hair and brown eyes were kind of boring, but he thought he'd at least be considered passably good-looking.

He leaned over and whispered in her ear, "Thank you, Sarah."

"Oh don't worry, cowboy, when I need you, I'll let you know."

When they stepped in, Sarah was once again the sexy kitten that he'd seen at the saloon. The sheriff rose, knocking his chair back. He stood about Zeke's height, thin as a rail with steel gray hair and beard. The tin star gleamed on his blue shirt.

"Miss Sarah!"

"Well, hello there, Jimmy Turner. You haven't stopped in lately. I've missed you." She sashayed over and Zeke moved back to enjoy the show.

"Who's your friend?"

"Oh, that's Mr. Blackwood. He's come to pick up your prisoner. Apparently some sort of mix-up with Marvin and the store. I just met Mr. Blackwood at the door while I was on my way in to see you." She smiled widely.

"Mix-up? There was a mix-up?" The poor sheriff appeared completely confused. He peered at Zeke, who took his hat off and did his best to look trustworthy.

"Afternoon, Sheriff."

"What kind of mix-up was it?"

Sarah flapped her right hand in the air. "Oh, you know Marvin. He's always looking for an excuse to poke fun at someone or tell some gossip." She sat on the edge of the desk and leaned forward.

The sheriff was treated to a clear view of the cleavage that nearly spilled from her bodice.

"When are you going to come over and see me?"

While the sheriff's eyes were glued to her chest, she picked up the keys from the desk and held them out behind her. Zeke gratefully took them and walked to the back, hoping he didn't appear too anxious.

"Well, you know Sally doesn't like me going to the saloon, especially if I go to play poker. She likes her pin money."

"I'm sorry to hear that, Jimmy. I surely have been missing you."

Zeke smothered a chuckle as he stepped into the back of the jail where the cells were located. There were four of them. One held a snoring, dirty man on a cot. The other, a grinning Jake who clutched the bars.

"About time one of you got here."

"We had a piece of luck running into Miss Sarah at the saloon. If it weren't for her I wouldn't be here with the key in my hand."

"Hurry up then."

"Hold your water, Sheridan. I'm coming." Zeke unlocked the cell and Jake darted out.

"Thank God. Thank God."

Zeke politely ignored the trembling in his friend's hands. He understood more than most people would how hard it was for any of them to be in a cell, to be behind bars.

"Let's get going before the sheriff gets his face out of her tits."

Jake snickered as they walked out. Sarah held out her hand and Zeke returned the keys to her palm.

"Thank you kindly, Sheriff. Hope you have a wonderful evening," Zeke called out.

When the door closed behind them, Zeke held his breath, waiting for the lawman to shout. All he heard was the tinkling of Sarah's laughter.

"Let's get you the hell out of town."

"Don't have to tell me twice." Jake stretched and smiled broadly.

They returned to the saloon at a brisk pace. "Where's your horse?"

"I heard the sheriff tell that bastard Nessman that he put it up at the livery." Jake curled his lip in anger.

"Take my horse and head back to camp. I'll get yours. No need for you to be in town one second longer than necessary."

Jake's blue gaze locked with Zeke's. "I don't know how to tell you how much...I mean, I didn't know..."

Zeke put his hand on his friend's shoulder. "Once a Devil, always a Devil. Now get moving before anyone sees you. That red hair of yours is like a goddamn bonfire."

Jake grinned. "I can't help it. My daddy liked redheads." He hopped on the horse and did his best to hurry down the street without actually galloping.

Zeke made sure Jake was out of sight and on his way back to safety before heading down to the livery to get Jake's horse. Later on, Zeke would have to come back and give Sarah a proper thank you.

ഔരു

Nate rode as fast as he could push Bonne Chance. He was a good horse, but he did have limits. Nate didn't feel comfortable leaving things the way they were in Grayton. Jake unaccounted for, Gideon recovering from a gunshot wound—a minor one but still a gunshot wound—and Elisa putting her entire future in Nate's hands.

Not a neat and tidy situation. All of it made Nate's skin itch. He wanted to put some things in order, so many things were as yet unfinished and confusing. He hoped that his trip to Bellridge would be just the thing to get everything back to where it needed to be.

By the time he made it to the city, it was past six o'clock in the evening. No hall of records would be open at that time of day. Even if it was closed, Nate took the time to locate the hall of records, which happened to be in the same building with the county courthouse. It was near the center of town, with plenty of businesses surrounding it.

Nate knew he'd have to bunk down and wait for the morning. He decided to spend a little money and get a room at the hotel he found near the hall of records. After paying a dollar for a room and bath for the night, Nate headed for a drink in a saloon, anything to calm his nerves, to try to get rid of the jittery feeling that wouldn't leave him.

When he returned to the hotel room, he lay in bed staring at a stain on the ceiling. For a reason that baffled him, he couldn't stop thinking about Elisa and the last time they'd been together. The way she'd ridden him had brought him intense pleasure. It was the same act he'd done with various women, but it felt different. Very different.

Nate was afraid he was falling in love with her. After he admitted that to himself, panic sank its claws into him.

What would he do if he fell completely in love with her? The Devils hadn't planned on staying in Grayton very long. Getting involved with Elisa certainly complicated things.

Nate didn't like complicated because it was unpredictable, therefore out of his control.

ℰᴑᏻ

It seemed as though he'd just been able to fall asleep when the sun streamed through the window, calling him to wake up. Nate took extra care to make sure all of his clothing was neat and clean. He'd brought his best shirt and trousers, best of course being a relative word, and brushed his jacket clean.

Although it was breakfast time, he didn't think he'd be able to eat anything. As he left the hotel room with his saddlebags in hand, he reconsidered. He knew he'd have to have something in his stomach or risk it yowling at an inopportune moment. His mission was to appear as a successful business man. A successful businessman should not have a growling stomach.

He headed downstairs and left the key on the front counter. "Much obliged." He nodded to the desk clerk. "Room three."

The hotel conveniently enough had a restaurant attached to it. He was able to walk right through a doorway and into the dining area. He sat at a small empty table and tried his best to look as if he wasn't worried to death. His stomach cramped and he forced himself to breathe in and out slowly.

Those few precious minutes allowed him to seize control of the runaway panic that constantly threatened him. The waitress appeared, probably no older than Elisa. An average-looking young woman with curly brown hair and brown eyes, she likely didn't worry too much about being murdered in her bed or having her cattle rustled.

The pang of missing Elisa hit him straight in the gut. How he could miss her in such a short period of time was a mystery. This waitress didn't even resemble Elisa, yet here was Nate acting like a lovesick idiot.

"Good mornin', sir." Dammit to hell, she even had an Irish accent. Another reminder of the Taggert family.

"Good morning," he forced out. "Coffee please with two biscuits and jam." He didn't think his stomach would be able to handle anything more complicated than that.

"Right away, sir."

As she moved off to fulfill his breakfast order, Nate fingered the copy of the bill of sale that he kept in his coat pocket. Hell he'd even slept with it under the pillow, just in case. He didn't put it past O'Shea to have Nate followed. He'd checked as he traveled and didn't see anyone. That didn't mean anything other than if someone was tracking him, he had very good tracking skills.

Nate's breakfast arrived within minutes. He ate the biscuits and drank the coffee without tasting anything, but it was enough to satisfy his body. Now he could get on to what he really wanted to do—get to the hall of records.

As he paid for the food, Nate asked the waitress, "Do you know what time it is?"

"Oh, it's just past eight. I know that because Nonny, the man who brings by the milk, just left and he always gets here right before eight."

"Thank you. I hope you have a wonderful day."

A sweet shade of pink spread across her cheeks and Nate realized the young girl assumed he'd been flirting with her. She needn't have worried. His mind and body could only focus on one woman.

Nate walked to the livery where he'd stabled Bonne Chance. After removing his folio, he secured his saddlebags with his tack. Every successful businessman had a folio, but didn't carry around his traveling bags. By the time he arrived at the hall of records, it had to be nearly eight-thirty.

He hoped it was open. When he saw a man exiting the building, he breathed an inner sigh of relief. If someone was leaving, it meant Nate could finally get what he came for. He entered the building and found the records room without a problem.

The person working behind the counter was an older man with graying hair, wiry sideburns, droopy eyes and a clean but wrinkled brown suit. He sat on a stool stamping documents. Several piles in various heights were arranged around him.

Nate sized him up and formulated his battle plan to achieve his goal. He reached into his pocket and pulled out a small paper bag of horehound candy. Smiling, he set down his folio with the candy sitting on top.

"Good morning, sir."

"What? Oh, yes, yes, good morning. Are you sure you're in the right place, young man?" The impatience in his voice matched the annoyance in his eyes.

Nate glanced around. "If this is the hall of records, then I'm definitely in the right place." He held out his hand. "Nathaniel Marchand of D.H. Enterprises."

The older man eyed the outstretched hand for a moment or two before shaking it briefly. In that short interval, Nate determined that at some point in time, this man had done manual labor. Calluses upon calluses graced his palm. Obviously someone who was intelligent, learned and wasn't afraid to do hard work. Perfect.

"William. William Baker."

"Mr. Baker, I'm here on behalf of my client, Mr. Samuel O'Shea. Perhaps you've heard of him."

A small nod.

"We're looking to put a particular piece of property up for sale. The former owners of this property have been, shall I say, difficult in giving up said property. Mr. O'Shea wants to be sure the correct paperwork has been filed in the hall of records for the county." Nate's palms started sweating as the lies rolled off his tongue.

He gazed behind Mr. Baker and saw stacks upon stacks of cabinets and boxes in another room. He hoped like hell they were more organized than they looked.

"So what is it you need?"

"Well, several items actually. I'm wondering if they're filed under the parcel or by date?"

"There's this ledger over here. That's the information recorded by date when a sale happens. Back behind me"—he gestured with his head—"everything in there is filed by the town name and then the parcel."

Nate had hoped that was the case. This time his smile was genuine. "Do you think it would be possible for me to attain copies of the bill of sale, possibly the deed or any other type of papers you might have with regard to this parcel?"

Please, please, please.

Mr. Baker's eyebrows rose. "You sound like a lawyer."

Nate laughed. "No, sir, I'm not. Someday I hope to be though."

"I'd say you've got a good start, young man. I've got a heap of work to be done today. I can't be digging around looking for papers. You'll have to come back tomorrow. It's almost the end of the month, you know, and everything has to be done by then."

Nate felt his chance to get everything done today slipping through his fingers. He closed his fists and held on tight. "Would it be possible for me to look through the parcel records for the town? I assure you I will not touch nor read anything that is inappropriate. All I would need from you is the location of the records for the town of Grayton. From there I would be happy to look for the records I need."

Mr. Baker rubbed his chin with his right hand, smearing just a bit of ink on his skin. Nate decided against telling him about it.

"I suppose that would be all right. Let me just finish this stack right here and then we'll go in the back."

"And the copies of the documents? Will that be possible? I would be more than happy to assist." He sounded like an eager puppy to his own ears. He'd gone too far this time. Nate could almost feel Mr. Baker pulling away.

Mr. Baker glanced at Nate's hands that bore ink stains and calluses as did his own. "We'll see what we can do. I think you're putting the cart before the horse. After you spend time shifting through the papers and the dust, then we'll see about copies."

148

"Thank you, Mr. Baker. I can't tell you how much I appreciate your assistance."

"You should save that for your sweetheart. There's no need to be charming me."

Nate decided he liked Mr. Baker a lot. He sat down to wait for the older man to finish going through his papers.

Chapter Ten

Surprisingly, the back room that had looked so chaotic was actually in order. After Mr. Baker showed Nate where the records for Grayton were kept, he came across what he was looking for within two hours.

In fact, he found more than he was looking for. The deed, the bill of sale and more, including Melissa Taggert's will. The will contained information that might destroy Elisa, at best it would devastate her. Nate took meticulous notes in case he wasn't able to obtain copies, but really, most of it was burned in his head.

Elisa had been telling the truth. The bill of sale was not signed by Melissa. The will had the same handwriting that he had seen in the journal. The deed was only in Sean Taggert's name, therefore the sale was illegal on two counts. It hadn't been signed by Melissa, and she had no legal right to sell the property. That rendered the sale moot.

A double blow. Mr. O'Shea would not be happy.

The question was, what would Nate do with all the information? He rubbed one dusty hand down his face, then sneezed.

"Did you find what you were looking for?" Mr. Baker appeared in the doorway.

"Yes, sir, I did." Unfortunately or fortunately, it was found.

"You're putting everything back in the correct order?"

"Yes, sir. I made sure I marked the place where I extracted the documents so I could put them back appropriately." Nate felt like a schoolboy being lectured by his teacher.

"Excellent. I had a feeling you were the type of man who would do that. Now for those copies. I have a cousin two streets over who owns a printing press. In a couple of hours, you could have your copies, then bring them back here and I could stamp them as official." Mr. Baker rocked back on his heels, a self-satisfied grin on his wrinkled face. "For your boss, right?"

Nate told himself not to react to the lie. "Yes, sir, for my employer. I can't thank you enough. You've been very kind."

"I'm guessing you're a man who keeps things private so I'm not going to ask any more questions. In any case, you're welcome. Always happy to help."

Although Nate had expected the older man to be as difficult and curmudgeonly as he appeared, he was pleased to know that he'd been wrong. He looked again at the documents in his hand, and hoped that Elisa was as strong as she acted. She'd need to be.

By the time Nate left Bellridge, it was late afternoon. He had the copies and everything he needed. So why did he feel so empty? Probably because the simple task of removing a small family from a ranch had turned into a life-changing experience that Nate had not yet accepted.

So many dirty dealings, so much lying and deceit in one small town, it didn't bode well for the rest of Texas. It was too much. He'd survived the war only to fall victim to the greedy nature of man all over again. His mind whirled like a top as he rode, so many things crowded in his brain. Only one thing rested on his heart.

Elisa.

He rode the last five miles without even remembering that he'd done it. When the familiar outcropping of rock that marked the Taggert ranch came into view, Nate knew he'd already decided not to see Gideon first. He had to see Elisa.

෨෬

As she sat on her horse, Elisa's thoughts wavered between a smattering of hope that they might not be alone in their fight, to the nasty demon of doubt. Watching the herd wasn't too hard so she really had nothing to do and too much time to think. About Nate, about being with him, touching him, loving him. That was getting her nowhere but hot under her clothes so after an hour, she took to singing to the cows. They seemed to enjoy her rendition of "Barbara Allen" and lowed in return. Good thing about cattle, they didn't judge a person like folks did.

"You have a lovely voice," a man said from behind her.

Elisa's instincts kicked into gear and she whirled, pistol in hand ready to fire on whoever invaded her land. Nate threw his arms up.

"Darlin', it's me."

Her heart leapt at the sight, which was something she hadn't expected. In fact, her entire body reacted as if she'd been thrust into a fire pit. Trying to control the urge to gallop toward him, she scanned the tree line behind him for anything unusual.

By the time he walked to her horse, she'd grabbed hold of her runaway lust, at least enough that she could speak. Her traitorous nipples though hardened to the point of pain.

"Elisa." His voice coated her with its honey sweetness.

"Frenchie."

He smiled and she nearly smiled in return, but the haunted look in his eyes stopped her. "What's wrong?"

"You need to come with me, darlin', back to my camp. I've something I need to tell the Devils and you." His weighty words gave her pause.

"What is it? Did you find what you were looking for? Tell me." Her horse shied beneath her and she realized she'd been squeezing him with her knees.

"Not here. Please, come with me."

"But Da, he's finally on a horse. Look." She pointed at a distant figure on a horse on the other side of the herd. "He got on there this morning and insisted on coming out." This time she couldn't hold back the grin.

"Will he be all right alone?"

"Alone? You really want to leave now?"

He sighed hard and long. "Yes, Elisa. Now. I've already wasted an entire day. We're running out of time."

Elisa didn't scare easily, however she had a feeling whatever he wanted to tell her wasn't good.

"Why can't you tell me now?"

"I owe Gideon and the rest of my friends, and you, an explanation. I'd rather not do it twice. Please."

Elisa's heart thumped almost painfully. She had the overwhelming urge to kiss him until neither one of them could catch their breath. "Okay, let me just tell Da."

He nodded. "I'll wait here. I don't think he's going to want to see me."

She dropped a quick kiss on his lips before galloping off toward her father. Da's green eyes regarded her steadily. Just seeing him on the back of a horse still made her throat tight.

"Da, I need to leave for a little while."

"Is that him?" He gestured to Nate waiting at the crest of the hill.

"Him who?"

"Don't play foolish games with me, Elisa girl. Is that your man?"

Elisa gazed at Nate, sitting on the horse straight and tall. A sense of pride and something she suspected as the first beat of love raced through her. "Yes, Da, that's my man."

"I know I haven't helped with the herd much since I've been home. I'll stay here and keep watch." He cleared his throat. "You'd best do what you need to."

"Thank you, Da." She leaned over and kissed his weathered cheek. "I'm glad to see you on your horse again."

"Get on with ya."

Elisa wheeled her horse around and set off toward Nate. She only hoped whatever news he had didn't destroy the spark of life she'd found by just being with him.

ଛୠ

They rode back to Nate's camp in silence. Elisa's anxiety grew as they got closer. Not only was there impending bad news, but his friends would not be happy to see her. Especially since she'd humiliated them in a trap and shot one of them. It wouldn't exactly make them friendly.

"Don't worry, they understand about protecting your own."

She snorted. "Not likely."

"You shouldn't underestimate them. They might be a bit, ah, angry, but once I explain things, everything will be all right." Nate sounded sure of himself.

Elisa wasn't as confident. "I won't make you promise that's true."

He shook his head. "I think I'm beginning to understand you, sweetheart."

Sweetheart. Darlin'.

All of these terms of endearment made her squirm. Elisa wasn't sure what she wanted from Nate, other than the amazing sex. The thought of having more with him, as in a marriage, made her squirm even more.

The one good thing about trying *not* to think about Nate and their relationship, the time passed quickly. Before she knew it, they arrived at the camp. Four angry faces greeted them. Elisa hadn't had a chance to see any of them up close before. The rest of the Devils were a mishmash of colors and looks, but they were all tall and packing weapons. They were definitely a formidable group.

"Why the fuck did you bring her here?" the one-armed blond asked with a sneer that would make butter boil.

"Lee, let's be a little more gracious," the one with curly brown hair admonished, although his gaze wasn't too friendly. Then she noticed the bandaged shoulder. He must be Gideon.

"Like hell I will." Lee pointed at her. "That bitch shot you and got us all tangled up in that honey shit. I ain't gonna be polite."

"Well I for one have to admire her." The redhead smirked. "Not too many men have been able to get the better of us. Now this little bit of woman did it."

"Step lightly, Jake," the other blond one said through gritted teeth. "She didn't get the better of us."

"Oh, I disagree. Did you see how tangled—"

"That's enough. All of you." Nate dismounted and held up his arms to Elisa. "She's here as my guest and y'all will demonstrate that famous southern gallantry. Elisa was protecting her own."

The four men stopped grumbling and instead stared at her with a mixture of distrust, suspicion and downright murder. Elisa forced herself not to squirm under their gazes.

"Why did you bring her here?" Gideon asked.

"I found what I was looking for in Bellridge, and more. We all need to hear it together." Nate glanced at Elisa and she saw a flash of empathy in his eyes.

"Fine. Let's sit down and talk then, but don't expect us to open our arms and be her friends." Gideon gestured to the various logs and rocks around the fire pit.

They sat down, with the four men facing her like a jury. Nate sat close beside her on a log. She was grateful for his support.

"Elisa, this is Gideon Blackwood, Jake Sheridan, Zeke Blackwood and Lee Blackwood. Everyone, this is Elisa Taggert." Nate made proper introductions, which felt a bit ludicrous. However, every man tipped his hat to her, almost as if it were ingrained in their systems.

"Tell us what you found." Gideon appeared used to giving orders.

Nate apparently was used to hearing them. He pulled a sheaf of papers from his jacket pocket. "I found a number of papers filed with the county with regard to the Taggerts and their ranch. The first one was the deed, which is in Sean Taggert's name only. Then I found the bill of sale for the ranch signed by Melissa Taggert, although she had no legal right to do so."

"Her husband could have been missing in the war. Perhaps she thought he was dead," Jake offered.

"No, it wasn't even her who signed it. I found a number of other papers with her signature, and after viewing her journal, I can confirm that Melissa Taggert did not sign that bill of sale." He handed the deed and bill of sale to Elisa.

Elisa took them with hands on the verge of trembling. She couldn't focus on the words too well so she took Nate's word for it.

"What else did you find?" Gideon's expression had changed from distrust to interest.

"Melissa Taggert's will, a marriage certificate and birth certificates for Elisa and her brother." Nate didn't hand her those papers.

She had a feeling whatever was in those papers, she didn't want to know about. However that didn't stop her. "What's in them?" Elisa demanded in a cracked voice.

He sighed and whispered, "I'm sorry."

Nate shuffled the papers and held up the first one. "The marriage certificate is pretty straightforward, from October 1845. No surprises there." He held up another piece of paper. "Daniel's birth certificate from February 1851."

The third piece of paper rose slowly. "Elisa's birth certificate from July 1845." He set it on her lap and she stared at it.

July 1845.

The date rang like an out of tune bell. "What? I wasn't born in 1845. I was born in 1846."

The birth certificate beckoned her, daring her to prove Nate wrong. She swallowed hard and picked up the paper by the corners. There in plain sight was July 1845.

Impossible. Absolutely impossible. That meant she was born before her parents got married. She could not ever imagine her mother...and yet Elisa herself had had sex before marriage. Nate had even mentioned the possibility of a child, and she'd ignored him. Perhaps her mother had done the same thing, and yet her parents had been married three months after Elisa was born.

That was unlikely. No unmarried pregnant woman waited until the baby was born to tie the knot.

"Read it."

"I am reading it," she snapped.

"No, darlin', read it." He pointed to the top of the paper.

Elisa pushed his hand away. "Fine. I'm reading."

Elisa Marie Grayton

Female, born July 15, 1845

Grayton, Texas

Father: Samuel Adam O'Shea

Mother: Melissa Mae Grayton

Registered this day July 31, 1845

By Samuel Cook, Registrar

Oh dear God. Her vision grayed and she swayed toward the ground. Nate's strong hands stopped her from falling. Her stomach rebelled violently. She twisted around and vomited behind the log until there was nothing left inside her but spit and tears.

"Jesus, what does that birth certificate say?" she heard one of them ask.

"Something mighty bad by the look of her."

"Shut up, everybody. Give her a minute," Nate snapped.

Everything was wrong. Her entire world had just shattered around her and she could barely get enough breath in to survive. She wanted to howl and rant like a madwoman. She wanted to go shoot Samuel O'Shea through his black heart.

Her father. Samuel O'Shea.

Spawn of the devil, daughter of Satan! She wasn't even a Taggert anymore. Her stomach heaved again and Nate kept rubbing her back and whispering nonsense words. After a few minutes, the urge to vomit passed and she wiped her mouth on her sleeve. Only through iron will did she keep the tears inside. No way in hell she'd let Nate's friends see her bawl like a baby after they'd seen her throw up like that.

"Elisa," Nate whispered in her ear, "I'm sorry, honey. I wanted to tell you but I knew you wouldn't believe me without proof. I'm so sorry."

Oh, Da. Elisa realized the man she had loved all her life wasn't really her father. He'd only been her stepfather. No wonder Elisa didn't take after him like Daniel did. She wondered if he'd known who had sired her. Her family was not her family and never had been.

Too many unanswered questions crowded and jostled around in her brain. She sat up slowly, easing her head upright. Nate's kind dark eyes met hers, full of worry and love. It was enough to make her start crying all over again.

"What would you do if you found out the man you hated was your father?" she asked.

An indrawn breath and a couple of hisses met her question.

"I know you're upset—" Nate sounded too sympathetic.

She laughed shrilly. "Of course I'm upset. Now tell me what was in my mother's will. Don't think I forgot about that last document you've got."

Nate looked down at the paper clutched in his left hand. "Are you sure?"

"I'd rather hear it all at once. Better to have salt in the wound in one great big pile than a grain at a time." When her chin started quivering, she bit her lip to the point of pain.

Get it done, Elisa girl.

"Now get on with it," she ordered.

"The will is dated five years ago, before the war began. It states that since Melissa is a benefactor in Samuel O'Shea's will that should she die, her daughter Elisa Marie, inherits her portion. Also, the bank account in Houston also belongs to Elisa Marie, the balance in 1860 was six-thousand, eight-hundred dollars."

The redhead Jake whistled while Gideon's eyebrows rose. The angry Lee looked angrier, while Zeke looked unaffected. Nate's hand shook so much the paper rattled. He turned to look at her.

"I couldn't find a copy of O'Shea's will in Bellridge. I'm not sure why unless it was drawn up in another town. However, your mother had a bank account set up for you. I checked and there were regular deposits up until a year ago. The current balance is over eight thousand dollars." Nate cleared his throat. "If I were to hazard a guess, I think your mother received monthly stipends from your fa— from Mr. O'Shea that she deposited in your name. Perhaps she was planning on gifting you the funds when you got married."

"What are stipends?"

"It means your daddy paid your mama blood money to keep her trap shut about his bastard daughter." Lee looked as smug as he sounded.

"Shut up, Lee. Can't you for once see that someone else is in pain besides you?" Nate's voice was low and dangerous. "If you say another word, I swear to God I'll beat you into next week."

"Stipends are monthly payments, Elisa," Gideon said. "I think Nate's right about why and who. Apparently they stopped when your mother passed away."

That made sense. She couldn't have deposited any money if she didn't receive it. Did that mean O'Shea wanted her mother dead? Elisa had always suspected that he'd killed her. Perhaps this was the first step in finding out why.

"I think he murdered her," Elisa forced out.

"Who was murdered?" Gideon responded first.

"My mother. O'Shea's blood runs as cold as a mountain stream. There's no way he'd just give her money. She probably got it to keep quiet about me. He's a rich son of a bitch. Maybe he thought I'd try to take all his money." The possibilities of why were endless. Elisa had trouble accepting the fact that he was her father, even with the proof literally staring her in the face.

"Before we get into the details, let's discuss what we agree on, then we can plan what we need to do." Nate met everyone's gaze in turn. "Are we all agreed that the sale of the Taggert land was illegal, the bill of sale forged and that Samuel O'Shea is no longer our employer?"

Everyone gave their agreement, even the angry, foul-mouthed Lee.

"Good. The next question is, what are we going to do about it?"

৪০০৪

After talking for over an hour, they were no closer to deciding on the plan than when they started. Elisa finally no longer looked pale, and started looking like a red rose, an angry red rose. She and Lee butted heads constantly, and when Nate stepped in to stop it, he got his head bitten off by both of them.

Gideon forced them to take a short break from arguing. Nate walked to the stream with a fire-breathing Elisa. He could practically feel the heat coming off her skin. As they approached the spot where they'd first come together, his body heated.

He watched the gentle sway of her hips beneath the baggy pants. Elisa's scent teased his memory and the passion burned inside him to kiss her, touch her, join with her. It didn't seem the appropriate time, but he couldn't stop the thoughts from racing through his head and his body from reacting.

"What are you doing?" she snapped.

"Nothing. I just...I'm sorry. I don't seem to be able to stop it."

Her sharp gaze softened as she perused his rigid stance. "What are you thinking?"

"I'm thinking this is where we first, ah, came together." He glanced at the tree behind her.

"Mm, that's not what was on my mind, but now that you mention it." She ran a finger down his shirt. "I remember that day pretty well."

He shivered even in the heat of the afternoon. "Me, too."

She leaned forward and he pulled her close, the soft voluptuousness of her curves filled his hands. He hardened rapidly as her belly provided a sensual rest. Memories of what she felt like without her clothes made his palms itch.

"This isn't the best time to do this." He groaned.

"When has it ever been? Hell, my da heard everything the last time."

Nate shut his eyes to block out the image of Sean Taggert listening to them. It's a wonder the man didn't run him down with a shotgun. He wondered how much Elisa had told her father, whether he knew about their first encounter.

The possibility made his head hurt.

"What's wrong?" She nibbled on his neck, little bites that made goose bumps rise on his skin.

"Your father knows?"

She shrugged and pressed her breasts harder against his chest. "He's not angry. Da is a fair man. He just wanted to be sure you were honorable."

Nate's heart thumped. His feelings for Elisa were growing faster than a wildfire. To know that she and her father had discussed his honor put another angle on it.

"What did you tell him?"

She raised her eyes to his. "Kiss me."

An irresistible command. Nate lowered his head and when their lips met, he ceased to think at all. Soft, strong lips moved beneath his. Breaths mingled and tongues slid. Her stiffness melted beneath the heat generated by their bodies and mouths.

"Jesus Christ, what the hell are you doing, Nate?"

Lee's voice shattered the haze that had enveloped them. Nate stared into Elisa's now angry eyes.

"None of your business, Lee. Now leave us alone."

"Right. You're over here practically fucking this woman who tried to kill Gideon and I'm supposed to leave?"

Lee grabbed Nate's arm and the next minute turned into a blur of fists and cursing. He found himself on the ground grappling with Lee. All the fury, the hurt, the agony of the last four years that had been locked inside him exploded. He should've been surprised how well Lee fought for a one-armed man, but he wasn't. They had lived so long on the edge of darkness that it didn't take much to turn them into animals.

"Stop it, both of you!" Elisa shouted and yanked at his hair.

Nate ignored her and delivered a sharp uppercut to Lee's jaw. With a grunt, Lee head-butted him and Nate saw stars. It was a fierce battle peppered with fingernails, fists, feet, knees and teeth that nearly consumed him. Nate didn't remember feeling the absolute immersion in a fight since the beginning of the war.

The fight didn't end until a bucketful of cold water hit him in the face. The water was a shock and he completely let go of Lee and rolled to the right. He sputtered and spit out the muddy water. Someone grabbed his arms and yanked him away from Lee, who coughed beside him.

Nate stared up into a disappointed-looking Gideon.

"I sure hope you two got that out of your system because if we're going to fight O'Shea together, we need to stop fighting each other."

Nate glanced over at Lee who was in his brother's grasp.

"Same goes for you," Gideon snapped.

Nate felt like a balloon that had a pin stuck in it. It wasn't a pop, the air slowly leaked out and then his fury was gone, carried away on the breeze. He glanced at Elisa who stood on the bank of the stream, arms folded, eyebrows tented. Then he noticed the bucket at her feet. So that's who got them wet.

"Serves you right. Your friend here, he's got the right idea. I'm done fighting with y'all. I'm ready to fight together instead."

After shaking off the excess water, Nate walked back to camp with Elisa beside him.

"You know that wasn't very nice."

"It's what I would've done to two dogs that were fighting. What's the difference?"

Nate couldn't answer that because she was right. They had acted like two dogs fighting. He had at least a dozen, if not two dozen, stings, bruises, cuts and throbs all over. He'd been surprised that Lee hadn't said anything to the rest of the Devils about catching Nate and Elisa kissing.

Even if it had been childish and foolish, and he felt like he'd been in a fight with two men for all the fierceness Lee brought with him, for some strange reason, Nate felt better. Like a cork had popped and released the pressure. Maybe Lee felt the same way, which is why he hadn't revealed what he'd seen. Either that or he was saving it. It didn't matter to Nate if Lee told or not since everyone knew about his relationship with Elisa now.

"Company." Zeke's voice made everyone stop cold at the edge of the trees.

"Shit. Jake." Gideon spoke so low Nate barely heard him. "He can't see you. Go hunker down somewhere, we'll give you the signal when he's gone."

Nate had no idea if Nessman planned on arresting Jake again, but they couldn't take any chances. With nary a rustle of sound to give him away, Jake disappeared.

"Who's that?" Elisa asked.

"Trouble."

"I figured that. Friend of yours?"

Elisa put her hand in her pocket, and he knew for a fact she had a small derringer in there. He'd felt it when they'd been pressed together. Nate had been right—she had amazing instincts.

Nate grimaced. "Not even close. He'd like to see us all hang."

He stepped forward, tucking Elisa's arm into his. "Stay with me on this."

She nodded tightly.

"Good evening, Captain Nessman. What brings you out here?"

Nessman stood, reins in hand, next to the fire. He watched them approach. Nate glimpsed a flash of the fervor that drove the captain, the reason he was so dangerous. He honestly believed what he was doing was the true and correct thing to do. He *believed*.

"Apparently that idiot sheriff allowed my prisoner to go free."

"Your prisoner?" Nate frowned. "Why, Captain Nessman, what are you talking about?"

"Don't play games with me, Marchand. I arrested that redheaded thief in the store. He was supposed to be in custody. Apparently a pair of tits distracted the sheriff and now the thief is on the loose." Nessman made a grand show of looking at all of them. "Funny, I don't see him here."

"If you're referring to Mr. Sheridan, he isn't here. I wasn't aware there were any pending Army charges against any of us. How could he have been your prisoner?" Nate kept his voice steady, his enunciation crisp.

"While technically he wasn't arrested by the Army, he was taken into custody by me."

"Hmm, I see. If the sheriff released him, then I'm assuming the arrest was an error." Nate looked down at Elisa. "May I introduce you to Miss Elisa Taggert?"

Elisa took off her hat and her riotous hair tumbled down. The surprise on Nessman's face was absolutely priceless. He'd obviously dismissed her, hadn't given her a second glance, assuming she was man based on her clothing.

Nessman swept off his hat. "I beg your pardon, ma'am. Captain Elliot Nessman, U.S. Army, at your service."

Elisa, bless her wicked heart, nodded regally. "You're forgiven."

For some strange reason, Nate wanted to giggle. "Miss Taggert is actually under duress, Captain, and needs assistance." He glanced at Gideon, who with one gesture approved of the plan. "It appears that a local landowner is attempting to illegally seize her father's property."

Nessman's eyes narrowed. "What property?"

"The Taggert ranch. It lies just east of here. For the last year, Mr. O'Shea has been attempting to seize control of it."

"Don't you work for O'Shea?"

"Technically, we did, but not anymore."

Elisa expelled a breath, perhaps of relief, perhaps of frustration, he didn't know. She squeezed his arm and Nate knew she was behind him.

"After some careful research, we've determined that Mr. O'Shea forged a bill of sale. In fact the sale was made by the wife of the legal owner."

Nessman's frown grew deeper. "Are you saying that he made up a bill of sale in the name of a person who didn't even own the property?"

"It's more than likely that he assumed her husband was killed in action and that she was on the deed."

Elisa confirmed his assumption. "He was missing for six months."

O'Shea had seen his opportunity and grabbed it. Nate wasn't sure why yet, but he was damn well going to find out.

"Why am I supposed to believe a bunch of thieves and outlaws?"

"We're not outlaws. We were pardoned." Nate unclenched his jaw, reminding himself that if they wanted the Army's help, they had to play nice with Captain Nessman.

"Well I haven't pardoned you. I'm certainly not going to believe the load of shit that you're trying to feed me. Whoever signed it was probably one of those saloon girls and I'll bet every one of those documents is forged."

"Actually the gentleman at the hall of records in Bellridge, the county seat, has stamped them. They are not forged." Nate's temper warred with his desire to remain calm.

"More than likely one of you is good at making seals." Nessman's nasally northern accent echoed through the field. "Since I know you're not going to tell me where your friend Sheridan is, listen carefully. You will hand him over to me or I'll make sure all five of you will swing within two days even if I have to stage it myself."

He mounted his horse and with one last triumphant glare, Nessman rode off toward town.

"I guess we can't count on the army's help, can we?" Nate smiled at Elisa. "I'm sorry, honey. He's, ah, well, he doesn't like us very much."

"Really, I couldn't tell. No matter. I think we can take O'Shea down without that fool's help. Besides he probably has too much starch in his drawers to be any good with a gun anyway."

Gideon and Zeke laughed along with Nate, and he even heard a snicker from Lee. That was good. They all needed to be together to defeat a common enemy. United they stand, divided they fall. It was time to get united.

Chapter Eleven

Elisa returned home with a tiny flame of hope burning in her heart. While she didn't consider herself a damsel in distress, having five strong men behind her was a damn comfortable feeling. She never expected she'd actually convince Nate that O'Shea was a bastard. However, she should have known he'd find evidence of it.

Truth was, she'd doubted him, but now her heart and her mind had finally come to an agreement. Elisa trusted Nate. She spurred Midnight to a gallop and raced over the familiar ground while the wind whistled past. They were finally, *finally* going to beat O'Shea at his own game, legally. Elisa ignored the voice inside her that kept screaming that he was her father.

When Elisa crested the hill, the breeze brought something besides comfort. The sharp tang of fresh blood, an unmistakable smell.

Every inch of her body was instantly on alert. She leaned down and whispered in Midnight's ear, "Easy, boy, we need to be quiet."

Unfortunately, if whoever had spilled the blood was still in the field below her, they had likely already heard her. If she was smart and careful, she could get close without them knowing. When she left, Da had been watching the herd. It was still at least an hour or two before Daniel was due to relieve him.

Elisa wished she'd had the foresight to tell Da about the special call she and Daniel had been using. A hoot owl, one long, three short. It was a long shot, but she did it anyway.

"Hooooooooooo, hoohoohoo."

The silence screamed in her ears. True silence. She didn't hear any cicadas, no crickets, no night creatures at all. Something was very, very wrong. Elisa slid off Midnight and armed herself with knife and pistol.

"Stay," she whispered to the horse. For being such a fancy horse, he obeyed like a well-trained cow pony. She'd trained Midnight herself since her eighth birthday. He wouldn't move from the spot.

Elisa slithered through the dew-covered grass slowly, inching her way along, like a dog following a scent. She was glad the wetness masked her approach, not a whisper of a sound to give her away. Blood thundered past her ears as she crept forward. The smell grew stronger and she veered slightly to the left then reached out.

A sigh of relief threatened when she recognized it was a cow. Anger soon followed when upon examining the cow, she realized it had been left to die in the field after its neck had been slit open. She'd known the second that she'd scented the blood that something was wrong. With the discovery of the cow's carcass, it meant the trouble was worse than she thought.

Elisa's dry throat prevented her from swallowing. She grabbed a handful of grass from behind her and sucked on the wet leaves. She made her way around the cow, her trousers sticking to her legs. The dampness seeped through and soaked them, a combination of her own rancid sweat and the sweet dew.

She caught herself chanting, "Please be okay, Da. Please be okay, Da. Please be okay, Da," and nearly slapped herself to stop. The last thing she needed was somebody hearing her, particularly if they were brutal enough to murder cattle. There was no purpose in that, other than to hurt whoever owned them.

One by one, she found the cattle carcasses, slaughtered mercilessly. Most of them were still warm so it couldn't have been more than an hour since it had happened. Elisa wanted to weep in frustration when her count reached forty. Her back ached and her legs cramped. As near as she could tell, there wasn't a living creature in the field besides herself. That meant all two hundred cows were either dead or the rest had been rustled. Every bit of the future of the Taggert ranch had been decimated.

In the middle of working up a fine fit, she heard a moan. Her head snapped up. It didn't sound like a cow; it sounded human. Still keeping in a crouched position, she moved toward the sound, that small glimmer of hope that her father wasn't dead.

Unable to stop herself, she again repeated under her breath, "Please be okay, Da. Please be okay, Da."

Within two minutes, she found him lying on his back in a circle of dead carcasses. The moon shone on the dew covering his body. Beside him lay his horse, as still as the rest of the animals littering the field. Elisa touched his leg and it twitched.

"Da, can you hear me?"

She crawled forward until she could reach his face. The smell of blood clogged her nose as tears rolled down her cheeks unheeded.

"Da, please answer me." Elisa grabbed his hand, which was limp and lifeless, and pressed it to her chest. "Please, Da, please."

"Elisa..." he said in a cracked whisper. "I knew you'd be coming."

She leaned down and put her ear close to his mouth. "We need to get you home. I'm going to go get Midnight and—"

"No, I'm dying, Elisa... They killed them. Rodrigo and O'Shea's bastards killed almost every cow and held me back. Made me watch. They stabbed me, re-broke my leg and then broke t'other."

Elisa sobbed at the horror and pain he'd endured. "Oh, Da." She promised herself Rodrigo would feel the bite of her bullet soon.

"Be quiet now and listen to me. You have to take care of Daniel again. I'm sorry I haven't been there for you."

"It's okay. We were there for you. That's what family"—she swallowed hard—"is all about."

"You are my sweet Elisa girl. I love you, daughter. You have your mother's eyes. I wish I could see them. You promise me, *promise* me you'll take Daniel and leave. The land isn't worth your lives. I want to make sure that you're safe."

"Da, I can't promise you that. Please don't make me promise." Elisa's heart was being rent asunder.

"Will your man help you?" he said in a voice lower than a whisper.

"Yes, he will. He and his friends, all five of them, will help us. Don't worry. We'll be okay." She clutched his hand, willing him to live, trying desperately to push her own life force through his arm and into his body.

"Goodbye, darlin'. I love you, Elisa girl." With one last tiny breath, he was gone.

At first, Elisa couldn't believe that he'd died. She shook his shoulders, shouting his name. Tiny droplets splashed on her face and she realized it was blood, mixing with her tears. She wiped her cheeks with the back of her sleeve then put her face in her hands and wept.

Elisa threw back her head and howled at the moon. She'd never felt the kind of agony that swept through her at the murder of her father. Even after her mother had died, Elisa had grieved, but it didn't compare to losing her beloved da. She didn't know how long she sat there, weeping like a little girl. The cool night air reminded her that she was wet, that she knelt in the blood of her father. Around her the blood of two hundred cows mingled with the dew.

Death surrounded her.

When the overwhelming wave of grief finally subsided, she took several deep breaths to try and gain control of herself. On the heels of the paralyzing sadness came the hot, wicked need for vengeance.

Elisa stood, knife and pistol in hand. "All right, you bastards. If you're still out there, come and get me. I want to dance in *your* blood."

Nothing. Not a sound. Whoever had murdered Da and the cattle was long gone. She knew if she simply headed out to O'Shea's ranch, they'd likely shoot her before she could even get close to him. The old Elisa would've done just that, gone off half-cocked and angry as a bee's nest.

The new Elisa, the woman born from the shell of a girl, knew that her best bet to quench her thirst for vengeance was to ride with the Devils.

ഇൻ൚

Elisa headed toward home with the certainty that Daniel was okay. No way God would take away everyone she loved in one fell swoop. That would be beyond cruel and she couldn't accept the possibility. Midnight ran fast and true, his long legs eating up the ground.

The cabin lay dark, the sounds of the night protecting it. A good sign. The panic scratching at her hissed at the reprieve. Elisa dismounted fifty yards away and left her horse ground tied. She crept toward the cabin a bit more hastily than in the field simply because nothing seemed amiss. Yet she was still cautious.

Ten feet from the back, she stopped and hooted the signal. A minute passed, then two. Daniel could be asleep—he'd been working harder than a grown man. She crawled forward until she sat below his window.

"Hoooooooooo, hoohoohoo."

A bang, a thud, then the window slid open.

"Elisa?"

The sound of Daniel's voice was like the angels singing on high.

"Daniel, thank God." Her voice caught and the damn tears threatened again. She swallowed it all back with phenomenal effort.

"What's wrong?" He must've heard something in her voice.

"I'll be right there."

She ran around the side of the house. By the time she got to the door, Daniel was there wearing only his drawers and a worried look.

"Now tell me what's wrong."

When her legs gave out, Elisa nearly fell into his arms. "Daniel, they... Da..." Her throat closed again.

"Is that blood? My God, Elisa, do you have blood all over you?" He grabbed her by the shoulders and pulled her into the house. The room was illuminated only by the meager light thrown by the embers of the fire.

Daniel was more mature than any fourteen-year-old boy. He held her while her body shook with shock and grief, while she again wept buckets of tears. He stroked her back and waited.

"They murdered him. Those bastards murdered him and the cattle."

"What?" He stiffened and helped her up so he could look her in the eye. Da's green eyes looked back at her. A boy too soon a man, forced to grow up or die.

"In the field. They stabbed Da in the chest and slit the cow's throats then left them all to die."

Daniel punched his knee with the bottom of his fist. "Who?"

"Rodrigo and some pieces-of-shit mercenaries. O'Shea decided he was done waiting for us to leave." She took comfort in Daniel's embrace, grateful he was still there by her side.

"He's gone too far this time. I'm gonna kill him." Daniel stood with a look of absolute wrath.

"Not yet, Daniel."

"Why not?"

"The men who were working for O'Shea, the ones I caught in the trap? They're now on our side and they're going to help us. One of them even found proof in papers and such." Her stomach cramped at the thought of those damn papers and what they represented.

"Isn't O'Shea paying them? Why would they give up money for us?" Daniel scoffed.

Elisa hadn't thought about that. Why were Nate and his friends turning away money when they so obviously needed it? Nate's clothes were neat and clean, but even she could see the wear on them. The Devils had some supplies, but they were living in a camp, not at a hotel or at O'Shea's house.

"I don't know for sure. I think it's for honor and justice."

"That's stupid. Nobody does anything for honor and justice." Daniel faced the window with his arms folded.

"I do."

When he turned back, his face crumpled and Elisa found herself comforting him. Just like that he'd changed from angry man to lost boy. She held him tightly, hanging on to the last bit of family she had left.

§○○§

Nate couldn't shake the feeling that something was wrong. He glanced at his friends sleeping in the glowing embers of the campfire. Near the tree line, he saw Jake keeping guard. Nate had no idea what time it was but he did know there was no way he was going back to sleep.

He slipped on his boots and headed toward Jake. The dew-covered grass masked his footsteps. It seemed so peaceful, so normal, however Nate knew that was a sham. Life was anything but normal or peaceful. It was chaotic and frustrating.

"Couldn't sleep?" Jake said in a low voice.

"No." Nate sat on the rock beside his friend. "Something's wrong."

Jake stiffened. "What?"

Nate shook his head. "I don't know. I just feel something in here." He put a fist to his chest.

"Is it the woman?"

"What do you mean?" Nate wondered just how much Jake knew.

"I've seen the way you look at her, Nate, like she's your mate. Don't tell me you two haven't been together a lot. I can almost smell it on you." Jake chuckled softly. "Not that I blame you. We've been living like monks."

Nate grabbed Jake's arm and squeezed. "Step carefully, Jake." He couldn't keep the anger from his voice. No way would he allow even his friends to disparage what he and Elisa shared.

"Oh, so that's the way things are? I'm sorry, Nate. I didn't know." Jake sounded contrite.

Nate's anger dissipated. "It's okay. I know you didn't mean anything by it. It's just...I don't know. She spins me in circles one minute then brings me to the most intense pleasure I've ever had the next. A complete contradiction in everything she does." He ran his hands down his face. "At the same time, I can't imagine what I'm going to do without her after this is all over."

"You've got it bad."

"I know, believe me, I know." Nate sighed heavily. "I need to go see her, to satisfy this gnawing feeling that she needs me. More than likely, she'll laugh and shoot my hat off."

Jake laughed. "She does have that shiny quality, doesn't she?"

"It's one of the things I love about her."

The entire world paused as Nate heard the words that had tumbled from his mouth. Entirely unexpected, they hit him like a slap. He *loved* her? Nathaniel Marchand, the gentleman, loved a rough and tumble cowhand from Texas who wore men's britches?

Holy God. He did love her.

The urgency of his need to see her grew to enormous proportions and he couldn't wait any longer. Even if it was three in the morning, he absolutely had to go.

"I'll be back by sunrise so we can talk about the plan Zeke is dreaming up." He took off running before Jake even responded.

"Good luck."

Nate saddled Bonne Chance and was on his way within minutes. The horse seemed a bit put off to be riding in the pitch dark, but Nate took it as slow as he could to save his horse from a broken leg. A trip that normally took forty-five minutes, took about twice as long in the dark. At least that's what it felt like to Nate.

When he crested the hill and saw the familiar Taggert cabin in the moonlight, he couldn't stop the sigh of relief that escaped. Everything looked normal. A whinny from his right made him freeze. Bonne Chance responded and Nate realized that the horses knew each other.

"Elisa?"

When no one responded, he went toward the sound and found Midnight, riderless. Nate's stomach flipped and the feeling of dread slammed into him even harder. No way she'd let her horse be alone in the field at night. Too many predators, two legged and four legged.

He sidled up to Midnight and grabbed his reins. The black horse shied a bit, but quieted after hearing Nate's soothing voice. The reins felt sticky in his hands and when he pulled them up to examine them, his worst fears bloomed.

They smelled of blood.

With a pounding heart, he slid off Bonne Chance and did a quick search of the immediate area. No body, thank God. He did see slight foot impressions in the wet grass leading toward the house. Too small to be a man's. That meant she walked to the house. He whooshed out a sigh of relief.

Nate took both horses by the reins and walked carefully, keeping his eyes and ears open. The only sounds were made by crickets and frogs, with an occasional bat. If Elisa had left her horse out unattended, covered in blood, then everything was amiss.

The horses followed behind him without putting up a fuss. When he made it to the front of the house, he tied them to the cottonwood tree.

The house appeared dark except for a flicker in the window from what he assumed was the remains of the fire in the fireplace. He wasn't sure if he should walk in, but figured his safest choice was to knock. Elisa might shoot if he just walked in the door. Hysterical laughter bubbled at the thought. He hoped like hell she was able to hold a gun and shoot him.

He rapped lightly on the door. "Elisa?"

Several agonizing moments passed that allowed Nate to count his breaths and his heartbeats—the heart was definitely winning that race. The door swung open and a rifle greeted him.

"Elisa, it's me."

The clatter of the gun on the floor surprised him, but when she launched herself into his arms, he was overjoyed. He held her tight, thanking his Maker over and over for keeping her safe. When he'd found the blood, the horse, he'd thought the worst. Nate had lost so much in the last five years that losing her would damn near kill him.

His brain tried to wander off into what he'd do when their job was finished, but he closed it off with a snap. No need to borrow trouble, they already had buckets of it. He stepped into the house and closed the door.

"What's wrong, honey? I found Midnight—"

"Shit! I left him up there. Oh God, I didn't—"

"It's okay. I brought him home safely. He's tied up with Bonne Chance outside." He stroked her back, grateful to have her wrapped around him like a baby possum.

"Thank you, Nate."

Was she crying? Elisa was *crying*? His panic returned tenfold. "Elisa, tell me what's wrong."

Elisa told him in halting speech that her father and the cattle had been slaughtered in the grazing field. Left to die in the sweet grass, held by the moonlight and dew. Nate understood her agony all too well and held her tightly, grieving right along with her. Losing his father had almost destroyed him, he didn't want that to happen to her too.

"Ah, Elisa, I'm so sorry. So sorry." He sat on the sofa and cradled her on his lap.

"Are you and your friends really going to help us?"

Daniel's raspy voice startled Nate. He should have realized the two of them would be holed up together.

"Yes, we are. We made a promise to Elisa that carries to you as well. O'Shea is into some dirty dealings and we are committed to stopping him." Nate felt certain every word was the truth. There was nothing worse than a bully, except maybe one who used illegal means to gain what he wanted.

"All of you?"

"Yes, all of us." He held out his hand in the semi-darkness. "Nathaniel Marchand. You can call me Nate."

A moment passed, then two, until finally the boy shook his hand, showing a surprisingly strong grip for a young teenager. Calluses spoke as loudly as the trembling. He was a boy trying to be a man in a situation that would test anyone's mettle.

"Daniel Taggert. I suppose you realize you're holding my sister like a newborn babe. I should take offense at that, sir." His voice held no rancor, just exhaustion, anger and a touch of fear.

"Shut up, Daniel." Elisa laid her head on Nate's shoulder.

"You two should try to get some sleep. I'll keep watch until dawn."

Daniel grunted and snatched the quilt from the back of the sofa. "I'm keeping my eye on you, Georgia man." He threw himself into the overstuffed chair on the other side of the fireplace. Within minutes, he closed his eyes.

"I can't sleep, Nate. I...I need to get clean."

Nate hadn't mentioned the smell of blood because truth be told, he'd become immune to it. It used to make his nose wrinkle and his stomach clench. Now it was like any other smell on Earth...normal. He understood how she felt though.

The first time he'd killed a man in combat, the Yankee's wound sprayed blood like a gushing fountain. Nate was covered in it and spent hours in the creek scrubbing himself raw. He could still remember how the hot splash of the crimson liquid felt and the way it dripped down his hands.

"Let's get you a bath then."

Together they heated water on the stove by lamplight. Two buckets of hot, one of cold, then repeated it until the wooden tub was full. Wisps of steam rose from the clean water, beckoning like a siren. Nate started to leave the kitchen but she stopped him.

"Help me."

He didn't expect Elisa said that very often and he accepted her request with the honor it was due. He removed her clothes, which were crusted and caked with blood and dirt. After setting them aside, he picked her up and lowered her into the bath, careful not to splash the floor. She looked up at him with the saddest blue eyes he'd ever seen.

"He was my da."

"Yes, he was. No matter what any papers say, he raised you, loved you, and that makes him your father." He cupped her cheek. "Love is all that's important."

Their gazes locked in a moment frozen in time. Nate knew it was the wrong time for confessions but he couldn't seem to stop himself.

"You're confused, hurt and shaken by all that happened yesterday, and I don't want to make it harder for you. I just wanted to let you know"—he stopped and used both hands to cradle her heart-shaped face—"that I love you."

She blinked fast, her expression registering surprise and a smidge of fright.

"I don't expect you to answer me in kind, sweet Elisa. I just...wanted you to know that you weren't alone, that you do have someone who loves you." He kissed her lightly.

"Even if my father is a monster?" she whispered.

"Even if your father was Lucifer himself. It wouldn't change how I feel, honey. For the first time in my life, I'm in love." His hands shook with the force of his feelings for Elisa, as if his body didn't know what to do with so much emotion. He felt full, more than that, *overfull*.

Elisa kept silent, a first for the outspoken woman. Her eyes, however, spoke volumes. She needed him and Nate was too much of a gentleman to say no. He took the soap and a rag, dipping them in the warm water, his hand brushing the side of one full breast. His body wanted to jump in with her, but his heart knew it wasn't the right time. Now was her time to heal, to come to terms with everything that had happened that day.

Ignoring what he was washing off, Nate bathed her as he would a child, with care, compassion and gentleness. He massaged the soap into her scalp, using his fingertips to make her sigh in pleasure. The sound went straight to his heart.

He rinsed her hair several times, making sure every bit of soap was out and the auburn strands were squeaky clean.

"What will I do without him, Nate?"

They were the first words she'd whispered since he started bathing her. He poured warm water over her shoulders.

"Survive. Just as you've been doing. He raised you to be a strong woman, a strong person, Elisa. You'll make him proud."

Her breath hitched. "I feel so lost."

Nate plucked her out of the tub and swaddled her in a linen cloth. After she was dry, he scooped her into his arms and carried her to the bedroom. She didn't put up a fight or yell at him or even curse, so unlike the termagant he'd grown to love.

Her bedroom lay shrouded in shadows. Memories of the last time he was there assaulted him. He pushed the memories aside to make room for comforting. After tucking her into bed, he shucked his boots and clothing and joined her. Her warm, pliant body fit next to his like she was made to be there.

Nate knew the others wouldn't worry about him. He held her the rest of the night, keeping watch when she could not.

Chapter Twelve

Elisa woke with the first pink rays of the sun. Her bed felt too small, confining, as if something was holding her down. She wiggled and someone groaned beside her.

Holy shit.

She wasn't alone in the bed. The last day's events rushed at her like a brush fire, leaving her winded and scorched. Her entire world had turned upside down in the space of one day. She'd fallen apart too. Her, Elisa of the stiff back and ready gun, had melted into a puddle of tears. Nate had wiped the tears and taken care of her.

He'd also told her he loved her. Her heart thumped like a herd of stampeding cattle. *Nate loved her.*

What did that mean? That he wanted to marry her? Maybe he just said it because she needed to hear kind words. She dismissed that idea immediately. Nate wasn't that kind of man. He was too honorable for certain.

So he really did love her. A quiver worked its way up from her belly to her chin at the possibility of this amazing, smart, beautiful man loving her.

Of course he picked that moment to open his dark eyes, while she was being a crybaby. Again.

"Are you feeling better?"

She pursed her lips and willed away the damn quiver. "Don't know yet. I need to get up though. Daylight's already wasting."

Elisa jumped out of bed, belatedly realizing she was buck naked. He grabbed her by the waist and pulled her back into the bed until she spooned against him. His firm, rough body warmed hers and every inch of her skin jumped to life. Instead of being annoyed, she was aroused.

Apparently so was he.

"Nate, what are you doing?"

"Enjoying the last five minutes of being with the woman of my heart." His nose nudged her neck, raising goose bumps in its wake. "Before the second day of hell begins."

They shouldn't, really, but Elisa had a hard time convincing her body and heart what her head knew. She pulled away an inch, but the first touch of his hand on her breast sent her right back into his arms.

"I need...something, but I don't know what." Frustrated and annoyed with herself, Elisa pushed her bottom against his rigid erection.

Nate reached around and plucked at her nipples while he rubbed his erection in the liquid proof of her arousal. Within moments, she panted with need. Nate must've known what she needed and she gladly followed his lead.

He lifted her leg and entered her in one swift thrust, burying his pulsing staff deep. So deep. The pulse of pleasure radiated out from her core to the sensitized nubs of her breasts.

"Yes..."

Elisa let him take the lead, receiving everything he gave her. Quick, powerful, hungry. It was a mating, primal and elemental. She closed her eyes and simply let everything wash over, through and around her.

"Elisa," he whispered just before he bit her earlobe.

His hand crept down to her nubbin and he squeezed it between thumb and forefinger. Elisa almost shot off the bed as her body exploded in rhapsody. Tingles and sparks of pure pleasure traveled like fireflies all over her. She clenched around him until he shouted her name and pumped into her so fast and hard, she reached another peak.

She saw tiny stars behind her eyelids as she bucked and twisted in his grasp. His strong hands held her back against him and he spilled his seed into her welcoming body.

After a minute of heavy breathing, he kissed her cheek and whispered, "I do love you, Elisa."

She squeezed her eyes shut and tried to hold onto the feeling. Being with him, hearing him tell her he loved her. It would have to be enough.

Elisa knew it would be a dark day. The clouds were already gathering and they weren't in the sky. The few precious moments she spent in Nate's arms would give her the strength she needed to confront her father and avenge her da.

∞CB

Nate, Daniel and Elisa carried her father's body home wrapped in a sheet. The cattle stayed where they died, since there was no time to do anything with them. The carrion would eat well for quite some time.

Daniel and Nate dug the grave next to Elisa's mother's final resting place behind the house. Elisa washed her father's body then dressed him in his best clothes. As she combed his hair, her tears bathed him in grief.

Without a coffin, the best they could do was wrap him in the wedding quilt Elisa's grandmother had made, and lay Sean Taggert to rest beside his beloved wife.

Nate said a blessing over the grave while Elisa held back the sobs that threatened to burst from her. Daniel watched dry-eyed, eyes full of hurt and fury.

"Goodbye, Da. I love you." Elisa threw a handful of dirt over him, her heart a painful mess of agony.

Daniel and Nate filled in the grave while Elisa watched, clutching her father's hat. She still couldn't believe he was gone. Nate put his arm around her, the smell of man and sweat drifting by her nose.

"I'm going to go wash up, then we can talk about what to do."

"Good idea." She wrinkled her nose. "Even I can smell you and I've been crying for hours."

He chucked her on the chin and kissed her softly. "I love you, Elisa Taggert."

Daniel stomped off and Elisa knelt next to the grave. Content to sit for a while and say goodbye to her da.

೮)ೞ

"I ain't going." Daniel sat with his arms folded across his chest, a mulish expression on his face.

Elisa leaned over at the table toward him. "Yes, you are."

"You can't tell me what to do."

He stood and Elisa realized just how tall her brother had become. That didn't mean anything other than he looked down at her. His skinny, lanky body needed another sixty pounds to fill out, and the two whiskers sat lonely on his chin. Deep in his eyes, she saw the grief that she was sure reflected in her own. She understood why he wanted to stay with her, but she couldn't bear, could not allow the one piece of family she had left to be taken away. O'Shea already had too much to do with the first nineteen years of her life. It was time that she made the choices, not him.

"Daniel, Nate and his friends are going to help us. We're going to make O'Shea pay for what he did, but I can't do this if I'm worried about you."

"I can use a rifle. You know I can. You've taken me hunting before. Elisa, please don't make me go." He switched back and forth between man and boy so quickly, she had trouble keeping up.

"You're going to ride Thunder into town, find Sarah at the saloon, you know she was Mama's friend, and you're going to stay with her." Elisa kept her voice firm. She didn't think it was possible to have a dozen emotions pass over someone's face at once, but Daniel did it.

"You don't think I'm man enough to fight," he accused.

Elisa blew out a breath and frowned. "That's not what I said. I need you to be safe. There's going to be killing today, Daniel. I didn't say you couldn't do it, I don't want you to do it."

Daniel opened his mouth to protest yet again when Nate's voice cut through the argument. "When I went to war, I was eighteen years old. I'd been hunting too. I knew how to use a rifle, I even knew how to use a pistol. I could take one apart, put it back together, keep it clean and well oiled. I knew everything there was to know about hunting and guns."

Elisa turned, chilled by the haunted sound behind Nate's words.

"The first time I killed a man, I realized it wasn't like killing a deer. He was running towards me, not much older than I was. There was a lot of yelling and screaming, cannons firing everywhere, smoke and the sounds of men dying. And all I could see was this young man coming toward me. He raised his rifle but before he could get off a shot, I shot him. His head exploded like an old pumpkin somebody had thrown at the barn wall. It was hot and wet and it landed all over me. His eyes were blue and the very last thing that they saw was me pulling the trigger." Nate looked down at his hands as if he could still see the horror that had covered them.

Elisa wanted to touch him, comfort him, do something other than stand there like a fool, but she didn't. Nate had to finish what he needed to say.

"If I had to do it all over again to defend my honor, yes. To kill a man even once to protect myself, to protect those I love, yes. But I'm going to tell you one thing, Daniel. I couldn't have done it at fourteen because no matter how much you think you're ready, you're not. I had four years on you and it very nearly destroyed me." His dark gaze bore into the younger man's. "Let her protect you, that's her job. She made a promise to your father. Don't make her break it."

The air hung heavy and still in the small cabin. Daniel stared wide-eyed at Nate. Elisa wondered where the gentleman went who had made sweet love to her earlier that morning. In his place was a man who had seen the bowels of hell and returned. She knew at that moment that Nate was more than just in her heart, his soul touched hers. A soul that he had just bared to save her brother.

"I'll go." Daniel finally looked resigned to missing the confrontation with O'Shea.

Elisa hugged him briefly. "Thank you. Now you need to get going just as quick as you can."

After a tasteless breakfast of hardtack and coffee, Daniel seemed ready to go. He hadn't protested leaving again. Elisa reminded herself that she had to thank Nate later for what he'd done. He hadn't needed to reveal so much about his experiences, but he had just the same, to save her brother. They checked around the house, peering out the windows to make sure no one was waiting out there to ambush them. When Nate determined all was clear, they went outside and repeated the procedure until they were sure it was safe.

Daniel grudgingly saddled his horse. Elisa couldn't stop herself from hugging him again. Deep inside she hoped it wasn't for the last time.

"Be careful." Daniel glanced at Nate. "I don't know if I trust him."

"I do." Elisa was positive of that, a fact that surprised her. "I'll come for you after this is over."

"If you're still alive, you will." His young eyes couldn't conceal the fear of losing her too.

"I promise, Daniel. You'll see me again. I will come for you."

He nodded and scrambled onto his horse, then leveled a surprisingly mature glare at Nate. "You keep her safe, Marchand, or you'll answer to me."

"Don't worry, Daniel, I promise to. I'll keep her safe." Nate sounded as if he was making an oath.

Daniel accepted that oath with a handshake. As he rode off into the morning, Nate met Elisa's gaze.

"Are you ready?"

She harrumphed. "No. Yes."

A smile teased the corner of his mouth. "Let's go round up the Devils."

∞∞

Elisa and Nate rode side by side without speaking. His entire body hummed with the anticipation of battle, as it had a hundred times before. It was a state of mind that Nate had to achieve or risk mistakes in his actions. Control was important and it began with his mind, then his body and the actions followed.

The day had dawned bright and sunny, but clouds arrived to cover the sky. A silent omen that Nate didn't need. The horses' hooves sounded stilted in the morning air. There wasn't even a hint of a breeze and the stickiness felt cloying.

Nate kept glancing at Elisa until she finally snapped at him.

"Why do you keep staring at me?"

Embarrassed, he tried to think of a good reason, other than the truth. "Well, I, ah... Oh, hell, I'm just making sure you're ready, Elisa. You've never been in a situation like this and I'm concerned."

"Don't worry about me, Frenchie. I'm cocked and ready," she snarled. "Do you think I will fall to pieces like some ninny like I did yesterday?"

Far from it. He was afraid she'd get lost in the intensity.

"No, I don't think you'll fall to pieces."

"Then shut up about it and stop staring."

Nate kept his thoughts to himself but that didn't mean he wouldn't worry. Elisa had suffered too many shocks the last two days. Anybody, much less a nineteen-year-old woman, would be shaken by what she'd had to endure. His respect for Elisa had grown with each passing second.

"We're here."

His contemplation was cut short by Elisa's announcement. Nate was surprised to find them at the Devils' camp already. Everything had been packed up and the only thing waiting for them was the men and their horses. They were good at covering their tracks.

Gideon spoke first. "Everything all right?" His gaze probed the still pale Elisa, who sported smudges under her eyes.

"No, but we're going to make it all right. O'Shea's men murdered Elisa's father and their herd last night." Nate's fists clenched just thinking about the sheer brutality of the crime.

Gasps of surprise met his pronouncement. Every one of his friends looked shocked then angry and better yet, determined.

"Needs to have his balls cut off." Lee did not offer an apology for his language to Elisa. Nate actually agreed with the sentiment so he kept his mouth shut.

"Holy God," Gideon exclaimed. "Miss Taggert, I'm so sorry for your loss. Please accept our condolences on such a senseless thing." He was nothing if not a true southern gentleman.

Elisa didn't bat an eyelash. "Thank you. I appreciate y'all helping us."

"Is this going to change our plans?" Nate looked at Zeke then Gideon.

"Not really, although we won't have to worry about watching the cattle. You have any other family?" Zeke asked Elisa.

A shadow passed through her eyes. "Not to speak of. Just my brother and me."

Zeke nodded. "He head off to town?"

Nate sighed. "With a bit of coercion."

"So all we need to do now is bait the trap and wait for the rat to show up." Zeke handed Elisa a piece of paper. "Here's the note we wrote up to give to O'Shea."

She scanned the paper and Nate realized she had no trouble reading. Interesting for a rancher's daughter in small-town Texas. He was glad of it though—no one could take advantage of her because she couldn't read.

"You really think he'll come?" She handed the letter back to Zeke.

"I'm counting on it. If there's one thing O'Shea wants, it's his money's worth. Let's head over to your place now. Nate's going to deliver the note to O'Shea." Gideon glanced at Nate.

Nate had forgotten that part of their plan. He was afraid his self-control would be stretched to its limit by seeing the bastard who'd done so much killing. He'd be wise to keep his thoughts to himself, and perhaps he could convince himself of that before he made it out there.

Elisa turned to him with a worried look on her face. He cupped her cheek and forced himself to smile.

"I'll be back soon."

"Be careful." She squeezed his wrist so hard, he swore he felt his bones crunch.

"O'Shea has no idea that I'm not working for him anymore. I'm in no danger."

"Unless Captain Nessman told him."

Nate hadn't considered that possibility, but figured he didn't want to borrow trouble just yet.

He didn't have an opportunity to give Elisa a proper kiss goodbye, so he had to settle for telling her with his eyes that he loved her. She watched him leave, staring at him with a bucketful of courage.

Nate didn't know what was worse, riding away from his friends to a possible ambush or heading toward the man who'd caused so much grief and violence. Neither choice was palatable. He focused on maintaining his control and decorum, of not allowing O'Shea or his men to push Nate into revealing anything.

By the time he arrived at the ranch, Nate had his businessman mask firmly in place. He nodded politely to the men at the gate and continued on to Mr. O'Shea's house. Although he'd only been there once, he knew exactly where everything was. It paid to be thorough in research of county land records.

The dark-eyed man, Rodrigo, leaned against a column, watching them. "Marchand, you got news for Mr. O'Shea?"

"I'd prefer to give him the news myself, if you don't mind." Nate dismounted and made a point of tying off the horse to the hitching rail without haste.

"He's eating breakfast."

Nate pulled the paper from his jacket pocket, looked at it, then put it back in. "If you would, please let him know I'm here and that I have invaluable information to pass on to him."

"What kinda information?"

Nate managed a polite smile. "Important."

Rodrigo frowned, then whistled. A young boy appeared from inside and Rodrigo whispered in his ear. The boy returned inside at the same speed at which he'd appeared. Nate stood by his horse, hands folded, looking as if he had all the time and patience in the world.

The truth was far from the scenic picture he painted. His stomach cramped so hard, he almost had to tighten his belt. His teeth were about to crack from grinding them too much, and sweat pools were gathering beneath his arms. Nate kept himself under control, barely.

O'Shea walked outside a few minutes later with a napkin in his hand and a scowl on his face. "What the hell do you want, Marchand? If you ain't finished the job yet, then get outta here before I shoot you myself."

Not entirely unexpected, but definitely unwelcome. Nate switched his tactics to soothe the savage beast.

"My sincere apologies, Mr. O'Shea. I didn't think this information could wait. I found some legal documentation that might affect your legal claim to the Taggert ranch."

Although O'Shea looked ready to snap Nate's neck, Nate maintained his composure. He could see Rodrigo out of the corner of his eye, hands poised above the pistols riding his hips. The small hairs on Nate's body stood at rigid attention.

"Get on with it," O'Shea ordered. "My breakfast is getting cold."

"Well as you know, you hired D.H. Enterprises to remove the Taggerts from the property. Part of our service involves obtaining legal information to assist the parties in question to make the right decisions." Nate deliberately tried to sound confusing.

"I don't know what the hell you're talking about. So get to the point." Even though O'Shea sounded as angry as he looked, Nate saw a glimmer of interest in his eyes.

"If I may?" Nate pulled the left side of his jacket open and glanced at Rodrigo.

"Yeah, go ahead. He's not going to shoot you," O'Shea assured Nate.

Nate pulled out the paper he'd brought with him and tried to hand it to O'Shea. The older man waved his right hand in dismissal.

"I ain't gonna read that."

Nate surmised that he probably couldn't read. That was a shock. If he couldn't read, then he likely couldn't write. So whose signature was on all the documents Nate had uncovered?

"Well according to this, which was provided by your attorney in town, the Taggert ranch was owned solely by Sean Taggert. His wife, Melissa, was the one who signed the bill of sale, correct?"

O'Shea frowned. "I don't know who signed it. Alvin is the one who paid the Taggerts so if that paper came from him, then that's the right one."

"I see. Apparently Melissa's name isn't on the deed to the ranch, and since Sean Taggert was not deceased at the time of the sale, it renders the sale null and void." Nate took a risk. He had a hunch there was a whole lot going on here, more than just a greedy man trying to get his hands on a small ranch. Nothing fit together correctly—all the pieces were either too loose or too tight in this puzzle.

"What does that mean? I'm a cowman, boy. I don't know any legal mumbo jumbo, so stop using those big ol' words and just say what you mean. Spit it out."

"The sale of the Taggert ranch was illegal."

"The hell you say! There was a lawyer man and everything. I saw him write the check. It cost me two thousand dollars but I needed that water supply to keep my cattle healthy. Those bastards better have that money," O'Shea bellowed.

Nate's suspicion grew that O'Shea was as much of a pawn in the situation as Elisa and her family.

"Actually, Mr. O'Shea, the ranch was sold for twenty dollars." Nate hoped that cannonball hit its mark.

It did.

O'Shea's face flushed a bright pink. "That just ain't true. I paid two thousand dollars for that ranch fair and square. Are they trying to cheat and say I only paid them twenty dollars for it?"

"The bill of sale had twenty dollars on it. The Taggerts said nothing about the amount paid for the ranch." Nate waved the paper.

O'Shea finally understood Nate's implications. "Somebody cheated both of us. People who cheat me end up in a hole at the bottom of a canyon somewhere with their dicks cut off and their eyes plucked out."

Nate was glad he hadn't cheated O'Shea. He reminded himself to have an accounting of all the goods purchased at the general store and settle up with Marvin. O'Shea continued to bluster and shout while Nate listened patiently.

Warning bells went off just as Nate realized Rodrigo had disappeared. Nate knew the lawyer, Alvin Potter, had to be in on the swindle; he shouldn't have been surprised that the foreman was too. After all, he used to work for the Taggerts—he of all people knew the worth of the ranch. The situation just grew exponentially worse.

"I think I know who took your money, Mr. O'Shea." He inclined his head to the right.

O'Shea followed Nate's line of vision. When he realized Rodrigo was gone, the expression on his face was almost comical.

"Well I'll be dipped. That son of a bitch stole from me?"

"Mr. O'Shea, I think you should come back to the Taggert ranch with me, there's a lot that has to be—"

A rifle shot split the air. O'Shea grabbed his shoulder and fell backwards onto the porch. Blood splashed on the white column beside him. Nate hit the ground, the dust clouding his vision for a minute.

"Goddammit! He shot me. That bastard shot me."

At least Nate knew the Irishman was still alive judging by his complaints. Another shot pinged off the column to the left. One shattered the window directly above O'Shea's head.

"Stay down."

"I ain't going nowhere, stupid. He's shooting at me."

Nate crawled forward, hoping the next thing that happened wasn't a bullet in his own head. Men came running from everywhere, cursing and shouting.

"Look out, you fools. Rodrigo turned on us. Somebody kill that son of a bitch." O'Shea was nothing if not the boss.

No more shots were fired and Nate had a feeling that Rodrigo was trying to cover his tracks before he hightailed it out of there. Nate crawled up the steps and when he reached O'Shea, he assessed the wound. The bullet was still inside him, and from the look of it, he was bleeding steadily. He needed a doctor and soon.

Nate used his neckerchief to create a makeshift bandage, but the blood was already soaking through.

"I need to see Taggert." O'Shea's light eyes were glazed with pain.

"He was murdered last night along with his entire herd."

The surprise on O'Shea's face was real. Nate was rarely wrong about folks, but he'd been dead wrong about this man.

"Elisa. Did Rodrigo hurt her?"

Now it was Nate's turn to be surprised. O'Shea actually sounded concerned.

"No, he didn't hurt her, not physically anyway, but she's in pain for sure."

"I need to see her." O'Shea grabbed Nate's arm. "I *need* to see her."

"I think you need to see a doctor."

"Bah, forget the doctor. I need to see my daughter. I'm guessing you figured that out too."

Nate hadn't expected O'Shea to openly admit his paternity. "Yes, sir, we sure did."

"Does she know?"

"Yes."

O'Shea blew out a breath. "Then I damn well better see her now."

Chapter Thirteen

Elisa arrived back at the ranch with Nate's friends. They were all such an odd mixture. She liked Jake, he was funny and charming. She respected Gideon, he definitely was the captain of the outfit, but he never ordered them around, and yet he told them what to do. Elisa had never been in the Army before, but she guessed that was the mark of a true leader. Being able to lead your men and have them follow with loyalty.

Zeke, she had no idea about that mysterious man, he was as tight-lipped as a frog's ass. And his brother, well, Elisa had already made it very clear how she felt about Lee Blackwood and his big, fat, obnoxious mouth.

Gideon sent the other three out to scout the area and make sure no one was around. That left her alone with him. All she could think about was Nate facing O'Shea alone. Not only that, but he was doing it for her. He gave up money, and possibly his life, all for her. Just the possibility of someone doing that made her stomach quiver like it had a thousand butterflies in it.

It also made her heart thump and stupid tears pricked her eyes. She'd shed more tears in the last two days than she wanted to in a lifetime. She never wanted to cry again and here she was blubbering over a man acting like a knight in shining armor rescuing a damsel in distress.

Elisa didn't consider herself a damsel, nor did she consider herself in distress. That was neither here nor there. The point was, Nate gave up a lot for her.

"Nate has a deep sense of honor. He's very noble and loyal."

Gideon's voice startled Elisa. She'd been so busy staring out the window looking for Nate, she'd forgotten Gideon was there.

"You don't have to tell me that. I figured that out by myself."

"I knew you had. I just wanted you to know that Nate does things because it's the *right* thing to do." Gideon's emphasis was clear.

Elisa was about to tell him what she thought of his lousy opinion of her, but she didn't have the energy to fight with him. So she just acknowledged his words with a curt nod and turned her back to him.

She knew a lot about who Nate was inside by how he treated her and others around him, how he spoke, how he was always a gentleman. However she didn't know much about his life, where he'd been, where he grew up, other than the south somewhere. Alone with Nate's best friend, Elisa had a golden opportunity to find out something about the Frenchman who had invaded her heart.

"Did you grow up together?"

Gideon was moving furniture around, putting it in the most opportune spots to defend the house.

"Sort of. Nate's father worked at my family's plantation," was Gideon's vague answer.

"Worked? I thought he was a schoolteacher." Elisa forgot she was annoyed, her curiosity aroused.

"His father used to be my teacher. He'd bring Nate around with him so we had lessons together, Zeke, Lee, Nate and I. Jake came to live with us when he was ten, my mother's cousin's son whose parents were killed. My parents were good at taking in strays." A ghost of a smile touched his lips.

They'd been together more than half their lives. "You were in the war together?"

Gideon's soft expression hardened at the question. "Yes, we were." Three words, all crisp, with a period at the end that echoed in the cabin.

Elisa knew that was a topic she wouldn't pursue any further. It had changed Gideon completely; she wondered what it would do to Nate. Jake poked his head in the door.

"Three riders coming. Nate's with them." Then he was gone as quickly as he'd come.

Elisa headed toward the door and Gideon stopped her.

"No, stay in here."

"Listen, Gideon, I'm not one of your soldiers, your men. You cannot order me around. I will go out there whether or not you like it." Elisa would not stay in the house like some scared little rabbit. She pulled her pistol from its holster. "This isn't for show. I'm good and I can defend myself."

Gideon looked as if he wanted to paddle her behind and stick her in the corner. He pursed his lips together so tightly they became a white line. "I can't imagine what Nate was thinking."

That one hurt. Elisa didn't let the sting show, a skill she'd learned too well. "You'll have to ask him."

Gideon took off his hat and ran his hands through his brown curls. "I didn't mean that. I apologize, Miss Taggert. My shoulder is sore."

Elisa winced.

"It wasn't a very gentlemanly thing to say and I'm sorry."

"It's fine. But I am going outside."

With a sigh, Gideon begged, "Could you at least give us two minutes to figure out if it's friend or foe? If they have Nate as a hostage, you're going to distract him. If he has them as hostages, you're going to distract him. I need him to focus and he's done nothing but be unfocused since he met you. Please, Miss Taggert, stay in the house for two minutes."

Elisa understood his point. She didn't like it, but she understood it. Nate needed to have all his wits about him. If she went running out there like a silly girl, she might get them both killed.

"Okay. Two minutes. I'm going to be counting."

"I expected no less. Thank you, Miss Taggert." Gideon slipped out the door then poked his head back in a moment later. "Lock it." Then he was gone again.

Elisa cursed every man she could think of for being so damn bossy. They could use their manners and say please and thank you. She slid the lock into place, then stepped over to the side of the window where she could look out and not be seen.

The three riders came up to the house, riding hard and fast. One of them was most definitely Nate. If she hadn't recognized that beautiful horse of his, she would have recognized the way he sat in the saddle. The man knew how to sit on a horse.

Gideon met them over by the cottonwood trees. O'Shea was on the second horse. From what Elisa could see, there was blood all over the left side of his blue shirt, an ugly red splatter that made the situation even grimmer. Elisa gritted her teeth. If Nate had shot O'Shea for her, she'd refuse to allow him to go to jail because he was trying to help her. The third man she didn't recognize, but he looked like any other cowboy.

No one had their guns drawn, which was a good sign. That didn't help her heart though. She couldn't quite hear what they said, but after speaking for a minute, all four men looked toward the house. Toward her. Elisa's stomach dropped to her knees. She had a feeling whatever it was they were talking about, she wasn't going to like it one bit.

The snap of the lock made Elisa grit her teeth. She was nervous as hell. She closed her eyes, breathed deep, then stepped outside. Nate dismounted and headed toward her. The look of sympathy on his face nearly undid her.

Oh for certain she was not going to like what he had to say.

She glanced at O'Shea. What she saw in that old man's face had her heart pumping even faster. It actually looked like concern and something else she didn't want to recognize. She turned her gaze back to Nate.

"Is he your prisoner?"

"No, honey, he's not."

"Why not?" A question she didn't want to know the answer to, but she couldn't stop herself from asking.

"It wasn't him."

"What do you mean it wasn't him?"

"The ranch, your father's murder, all of it. It wasn't him. I know you're going to find that hard—"

"Hard? It's not hard, it's impossible. Of course it's him. It's his goddamn name on that bill of sale, his goddamn signature on all the papers we get saying get off the ranch."

Nate took her by the shoulders and looked into her eyes. "He can't read or write."

"What?" That was not true. Couldn't be true.

"You see that wound on his shoulder?"

"Yeah, good one." She told herself if O'Shea felt a thousand times the pain that her father had from his knife wounds, it wasn't enough. It would never be enough.

"I had a feeling, a hunch that something was wrong with our theories, but I couldn't put my finger on it." Nate cupped her chin. "It was Rodrigo."

Memories assailed her of growing up with Rodrigo watching her, feeling his eerie gaze on her young body. One of the reasons she started wearing trousers was to hopefully make men forget that she was a girl. Make Rodrigo forget. He smiled and charmed her mother, then left, disappearing and going to work for O'Shea. After Da went to war, all the trouble started.

Sweet Jesus.

Elisa had forgotten that O'Shea had been their regular neighbor most of her life. The last three years had been such an intense nightmare. The time prior to that seemed to fade, but now it all made sense. Elisa tried to absorb it but her brain and her heart had taken so many kicks the last two days, she didn't know whether to laugh or cry. She wasn't the devil's spawn.

"Does he admit that he's my father?"

"Yes he did. After we figured out it was Rodrigo and that lawyer, Potter, the fool Rodrigo ran after shooting O'Shea."

"Did you get hurt?" The last thing she needed was to have Nate wounded. He'd become the anchor in a world of confusion and hurt and anger.

"No, I'm fine, but he's hurt pretty badly." He looked back at O'Shea.

Elisa was surprised to see that the older man was not only pale, he swayed in the saddle.

"Why is he here? Why didn't you take him to the doc in town?"

Nate tucked her under his arm and walked toward the horses. "He wouldn't let me. His first and only thought was to make sure that you were okay."

She pulled away from him. "I can't. I can't. It's too hard, Nate."

"It's okay. I'm right here with you, honey. I'm right here." He held her hand, interlacing their fingers.

She gripped him tight enough that he winced, but he didn't make a sound of protest, as if he knew she needed to hang onto him as much as possible.

The thunder of hooves interrupted the conversation with O'Shea before it could start. When a rifle shot sounded, Nate threw her to the ground. Blinded by the dust they kicked up, all she could do was listen. She couldn't move with a two hundred pound weight keeping her pinned to the hard dirt. She heard a grunt and a curse, then the sound of a body hitting the ground. More shots rang out.

"Hell, he killed Joe," O'Shea grumbled from somewhere nearby.

Elisa figured Gideon had pulled O'Shea off the horse. Both Nate and his friend moved like lightning, fast and decisive.

Gideon spoke only a single word. "House."

Before Elisa knew it, Nate was half-dragging, half-carrying her to the house. His body continued to protect hers, like a human shield. She had no idea how he moved without actually standing or getting on all fours. The very idea of Gideon doing the same thing to O'Shea and his rounded belly made a hysterical laugh bubble in her throat.

When they arrived at the house, Nate reached up to open the door, then shoved her inside. She rolled like a hedgehog, landing near the table in the kitchen. She heard a slam and another round of cursing then all four of them were in the house.

"How many?" Gideon asked from his position near the side window.

Nate scooted over to the front window and peered out. "At least twenty."

"Another ten over here."

Thirty men?

"Who the hell is out there?" Elisa started to stand, but Nate jumped on her in a flash, pushing her back toward the floor.

His dark eyes were sharp and wide, nostrils flaring, a sheen of perspiration covering his face. "Rodrigo and his men are out there gunning for us. He's not looking for revenge, he wants us dead. We're the only ones who know what he's done. If he can kill us and make sure O'Shea is dead, there's no one who can point a finger."

Elisa had been confused and scared, but this made all that back away. In its place came pure fury.

"Let's kill that son of a bitch instead."

Nate looked surprised, then a small grin appeared on his face. "I love you, Elisa Taggert. Stay down until we figure out what to do, please." After giving her a quick kiss, he scuttled over to Gideon.

Elisa frowned. At least he'd said please. For now, she'd listen to what he had to say, until she decided not to.

Bullets continued to slam into the house, shattering windows and creating a racket that would wake the dead. Elisa considered going over to O'Shea, but for some reason, she didn't. She told herself it wasn't fear that kept her away, but she knew that was a lie.

O'Shea represented everything that went wrong in her life, from the moment of conception. Too many questions whirled around in her brain, not to mention the fact that her stomach was as tight as a fist.

"Please come here, Elisa." Nate gestured and Elisa gratefully crawled over to him.

Anything to avoid thinking so much.

"Zeke, Lee and Jake are likely waiting for our signal. As soon as we start firing back, they're going to hit them from the other side. You sure you want to do this?"

"Damn sure. I've been hunting for this family for three years, before that I always went with Da." She was proud of her skills with weapons. Gave her a boost of confidence.

"Is there ammunition in the house?" Gideon was loading a rifle in his lap, a Henry rifle.

"Where did you get that sixteen shooter? Isn't that a Yankee weapon?" She'd never seen one and wanted to try it.

Gideon's gaze chilled her. "I earned it. Now is there ammunition in the house?"

"For the pistols and the rifles. I don't know how much there—"

"Get the bullets and whatever weapons you have. Bring them here." Gideon set the now-loaded rifle down and pulled the pistol from the holster on his hip.

Elisa opened her mouth to tell Gideon to go to hell, but Nate's hand on her arm stopped her.

"Please do it, honey. We need to get an idea of what we've got."

She nodded and went to retrieve everything from beneath her bed. It all used to be kept in her parents' room, but after Da left, Elisa took possession of the weapons. God knew her mother was useless with them. She stuffed two full boxes, and one half-empty box of bullets into her shirt, then grabbed the two rifles and headed back.

When she got back to the men, O'Shea had joined them. She refused to look him in the eye. Instead she focused on Nate and setting out what she'd retrieved. He chuckled when she pulled the boxes out of her shirt.

"What? I didn't have a sack to carry them."

Gideon even cracked a small smile. "Thank you, Miss Taggert."

They quickly counted everything and divided them by three. Elisa was pleased the third shooter was her and not O'Shea. As they each gathered their supply of weapons and ammunitions, O'Shea finally spoke.

"You turning her into a gunman?"

Elisa leveled a glare at him. "You have no right to tell me what to do." She was startled to realize that she had the same chin as he did.

"You're my daughter."

She pointed a pistol at him. "Don't you call me that. You haven't done a damn thing for me all my life so—"

"I gave your mother money every month. Hell, I gave you that damn Arabian you ride. Your mother wouldn't let me see you. I tried to help you after she died, but you would have nothing to do with me." He wheezed and drew in a shaky breath.

"I'm supposed to believe you?" Her heart clenched hard enough that her damn toes hurt.

He pulled a stack of envelopes from his pocket. They had tattered edges and were stained with fresh blood. "Melissa's letters. Read them."

"Don't take offense, O'Shea, but now is definitely not the time for this," Gideon interjected. "Those men out there aren't going to give us much more time before they burst in here."

"You're right." O'Shea pressed them into Elisa's hands. "You keep these, read them when you can."

Elisa glanced at Nate who looked sympathetic. "Later, honey."

Gideon pointed at Elisa. "Take the post in the back. Nate, you stay on the east side of the house."

Elisa wanted to protest, but a window broke and another bullet flew past her head and embedded into the wall behind her. She decided to listen to Gideon, for the time being.

"What about me?" O'Shea grumped.

"You can hardly hold your head up much less a gun. Just sit there and stay out of the way." Gideon knew how to give orders.

Elisa crawled over to her post, ready to defend her life and her ranch. She gritted her teeth and pulled up every pinch of courage she had.

Time for battle.

ঙ০৪৩

The familiar sound of bullets echoed from outside the house. Nate had to keep swallowing back the coffee he'd had for breakfast that threatened to make a reappearance. He was distressed to realize his hands were shaking. The promise he'd made to himself to never kill a man again hung over his head.

This time he'd have to break it. It wasn't just kill or be killed. It was saving the woman he loved and his best friends. He could see Elisa as she crouched by the window.

"On my signal, start firing back," Gideon called from the front of the house.

Tension coiled inside Nate. He wiped his clammy hands on his trousers and his forehead with his sleeve. The rifle felt heavy in his grip, too heavy, but he lifted it to his shoulder and waited.

"Now!"

Nate peered out the hole in the window at the men milling around outside firing. He sighted carefully then squeezed the trigger. The man flew off his horse, landing in a cloud of dust. He heard Gideon and Elisa firing, then more gunshots from the tree line. Within moments, six men outside went down.

Rodrigo's men started shouting to each other and soon half a dozen of them were firing at the trees. Jake, Lee and Zeke must have heard the shots from inside the house and joined in. Thank God.

Minutes felt like hours as the firing continued nearly nonstop. The ammunition pile by Nate's side dwindled until only a handful remained. Nate took his time aiming and realized his sharpshooter skills hadn't waned with disuse. He was still as deadly as he ever was.

"I'm down to ten bullets," Elisa called. "You have any magic left in that head of yours, Captain?"

Gideon grunted. "I'm down to fifteen. No magic, but I damn sure hope Zeke does."

Elisa shouted in pain and Nate dropped the rifle. He crawled toward her as fast as he could. The sight of blood dripping down her arm made his vision swim.

"Jesus, Elisa!"

"It's just a graze. I'm fine. Wrap it up with your neckerchief or something."

He felt panic clawing at his back as each drop of blood fell to the wooden floor. "I used it on your fa— on O'Shea."

"Then use mine. Just make it fast." She squeezed her eyes shut and held her hand like a tourniquet on the wound.

Nate tried three times to get the knot undone on the cloth before Gideon pushed him out of the way and easily untied the neckerchief.

"She's going to bleed to death before you figure this out. Snap out of it, Nate."

A sharp slap to the face brought Nate back from the dark place he'd tumbled into. He stared into Gideon's blue eyes. "Jesus, I'm sorry, Gid." He trembled with the emotions battering him.

Gideon shook his head. "It's okay. We're on borrowed time from the devil anyway. Might as well spend it trying to fight the old son of a bitch."

"You two are crazier than bed bugs." Elisa picked up the rifle and went back to her post.

Nate wiped blood off his lip where his teeth had cut in from Gid's slap. "It looks bad, Gid. I've only got a couple shots left."

Gideon frowned. "Me too."

"Hello the house!" Rodrigo shouted from outside. "I've got someone out here who wants to say something."

Nate and Gideon looked at each other with equal expressions of surprise. They scuttled back to the front of the house and looked out the windows from their posts.

Jake was on his knees in front of Rodrigo, half his face covered with blood. Rodrigo had him by the hair, a shotgun shoved in his ear.

"Oh my God," Nate gasped.

"Don't you listen to him, Gideon," Jake called. "I'll come back from the grave to haunt you if you give in to this idiot."

Rodrigo kicked him in the kidneys and Jake fell to his hands. Gideon crawled toward the door and Nate shook his head.

"Don't."

"I can't let him die like that, Nate." Gideon's voice was full of pain and fury.

Nate glanced back at Elisa. "Neither can I." He grabbed the door handle and pulled.

"Nate!" Gideon lunged at him, but Nate moved too fast.

A dozen guns pointed at him. He could hear Elisa and Gideon shouting from inside the house. All he could focus on was his friend in pain, risking his life because Nate asked him to. There was no way on God's green Earth that Nate would let Jake suffer.

"Let him go."

"Ah, the smooth talker." Rodrigo kicked Jake. "I had a feeling we might see each other again."

"If you kick him one more time, I'll kill you myself." Nate kept a tight rein on the fury that threatened to overcome him.

"Big words for a man who could die if I blink." Rodrigo smiled that charming grin that probably got him untold things in his lifetime.

"There are four rifles trained on your head at this very second, Rodrigo. All I need to do is move my hand a certain way and your brains decorate the dust behind you." Nate clenched his fists and willed the control to stay for just a bit longer.

"Why did you come out here, fancy boy?" Rodrigo waved his pistol around. "Why couldn't you just let us kill the boy and the little bitch and go away with money in your pockets from O'Shea?"

"My friends and I may work for whoever will pay us, but that doesn't mean we'll kill for them. You've murdered at least two people and an entire herd of cows to get your hands on O'Shea's money. That ends here and now. Today is your last day, Rodrigo." Nate took a step forward. "The Devils are going to stop you."

"What Devils? What are you talking about?" Rodrigo glanced around. "That redhead is some kind of *bruja*, but I don't think she called up no demons."

Nate's smile was as cold as Rodrigo's heart. "You're looking at one." He raised his right arm and let loose a rebel yell that would do Lee proud.

Nate dropped to the ground and grabbed Jake by the collar. Bullets sang around them, kicking up dust and dirt. Confusion and chaos surrounded them as Nate pulled his friend toward the house. A sharp sting on his ass told him at least one bullet hit its mark.

The sounds of more horses made his heart sink. Jake gained momentum and together they made their way toward the front door. When they were close enough, Gideon reached out and yanked them in.

"Oh, shit, I'm hit," Jake cried out. "Son of a bitch. My leg!"

"It's Daniel and the sheriff." Elisa appeared next to them, her face aglow with excitement. "I see them coming. He's got at least fifteen men with them."

"Thank God." Nate rested his forehead on the floor, breathing in the dirt and dust like it was the sweetest ambrosia.

"As for you, I'll talk to you later about that stupid thing you just did." Elisa punched him in the arm hard enough to knock him over.

Gideon snickered and Jake managed a strangled chuckle.

"Shut up." Nate crawled toward the window, grateful for Daniel's insistence on not listening. Without that kid and the sheriff, he didn't think they would have survived the day.

It wasn't a good day to die.

They continued to shoot from inside the house, but sparingly. In the melee, they didn't want to shoot one of the men who'd come to assist them. Rodrigo's men began to fall in earnest. Within ten minutes, those who hadn't run off were in custody.

Except Rodrigo.

"Where is he?" Gideon called.

"I don't know. I don't see him." Nate ran toward the back of the house, where there was only one small window. As he came around the corner, he ran full force into someone. They both grunted and Nate fell backwards with the other person on top of him.

He stared up into Rodrigo's furious gaze. Blood dripped from wounds on his face and arm.

"I worked for years to get close to that old man. Did everything he asked me to, scraped and bowed like a slave. And you took everything."

Too late Nate realized the pressure on his neck was a knife. Damn, he walked into this without his usual careful actions. He'd so wanted to have the opportunity to marry Elisa and see her grow big with his child.

Pain came first as the knife started to slide across his skin, then it stopped and Rodrigo let loose a scream that made Nate's ears ring. Elisa stood above them, blood covering her hands. Rodrigo clutched at his back and rolled off Nate.

"You stabbed me, you bitch."

Rodrigo lunged to his feet, knife in hand and ran toward Elisa. She whipped her gun out of its holster and shot him between the eyes. Blood, brain and bone spattered over Nate. The urge to vomit overwhelmed him, and he turned on his side and retched.

Elisa's strong hands rubbed his back. "It's okay, Frenchie. I got him. He's gone."

Nate wasn't afraid of dying. It was the killing that did him in. Elisa would understand that as soon as the full impact of what she'd done settled on her shoulders. He wiped his face with his sleeve and got to his knees.

Their arms wrapped around each other and Nate felt the return of sanity.

"You're bleeding like a stuck pig. We need to get you some bandages." She squeezed his behind. "Hell's bells, they shot you in the ass? Those bastards." Elisa pulled back and looked him in the eye. "We did it."

"Yeah, honey, we sure did."

He noticed Gideon in the doorway with a bloody Jake by his side. "Doctor's office anyone?"

They all laughed, breaking the tension.

"Let's let the sheriff take care of the rest of these sons of bitches. We need to pile in the wagon and get to town before half of you die on me." Gideon and Jake disappeared from view.

"I love you, Nate."

Elisa's soft voice made Nate's heart hiccup. "What?"

"You heard me. I love you, stupid man. Now tell me you love me before I punch you again." Her blue eyes brimmed with emotion, everything from love to fear to relief.

"I love you, honey. You know I do." He hugged her so tightly, his arms shook.

"Now let's get you cleaned up and into town to the doc. God knows he's going to make a fortune from this crew." She grinned. "Now I've got to go paddle some fourteen-year-old behind."

She helped Nate to his feet and a wave of pain hit him. Going to the doctor was sounding better and better. When they emerged from the bedroom, they found Gideon crouched next to O'Shea.

"He's unconscious, and his pulse is thready. We need to leave now."

Elisa's grip tightened to the point of pain on his arm. "I'll hitch up the wagon."

She ran out the door, red locks flapping behind her.

"I don't think he's going to make it," Gideon confessed to Nate.

Nate was afraid of what that would do to Elisa. She'd lost so much in the last year, he didn't know what she'd do if she lost the father she'd just found.

Chapter Fourteen

Elisa stepped outside and found the aftermath of battle. She was expecting it, but it was still a shock. Growing up on a ranch got a person used to seeing blood and life's beginning and end. This, however, was something completely outside her experience.

Her stomach rolled and heaved at the amount of blood staining the ground and grass. The Earth absorbed it as if it was thirsty. Elisa couldn't contain the shudder at the thought of all the killing that went on just because of one man's greed. A man she had killed.

She'd been shooting at the men just as Nate and his friends were, but the strangers had been far enough away that all she saw were bodies falling during the battle. Killing Rodrigo was easy in the second it took her to do it. He was about to murder the man she loved. Her brain didn't have to work, just her body. Afterwards when Nate was covered in the gore from it, she realized just how much it would affect her. Killing wasn't for the faint of heart.

It would be a day forever etched in her memory, a day that would change who she was. Elisa had considered herself grown before meeting Nate, now she knew differently. The image of pulling that trigger would never leave her. Neither would the carnage outside.

"Elisa!" Daniel rushed at her, arms spread wide.

She opened hers and hugged the stuffing out of him. "Daniel, you took ten years off my life when I saw you riding in with the sheriff. Don't you listen?" She pulled back and punched him in the jaw.

He reared back while she dealt with the pain in her knuckles.

"Ouch. Dammit, what was that for?"

"For not listening. From now on, Daniel Sean Taggert, you're going to listen to me." She grabbed his arm. "Now help me get the wagon hitched up. We've got a passel of hurt folks who need the doc."

Including my father.

After a brief conversation with the sheriff, Elisa and Daniel made it to the barn. Together, they had the horses hitched quickly and pulled the wagon up to the house. Gideon and Zeke carried O'Shea out, while Lee helped Jake. Nate followed, limping and holding a piece of linen to his neck. His dark hair was matted with blood and his face a mass of bruises and cuts, but he looked beautiful.

Elisa smiled and he climbed up on the wagon next to her. He hissed when his bottom hit the hard wooden seat.

"Daniel, get that pillow from my room."

Daniel, duly chastised from his run-in with his sister's fist, ran in the house and appeared moments later with the embroidered pillow her mother had made her work on. The stitches were crooked and the pattern wrong, but she'd kept it as a reminder of what she shouldn't ever do again.

"Lift up."

Nate raised a brow. "You want me to sit on your pillow?"

"Yes, stupid man. It will staunch the bleeding and help ease the pain, now lift up." She shoved the pillow under him then he sat back down again.

"That does feel better."

"See?" She glanced behind her, ignoring Nate's impatient look.

Nate's four friends sat around O'Shea like a human pillow, positioned to keep him as stable as possible. Gideon nodded at her.

"Hiyah!" She got the horses in motion and prayed they'd make it in time.

When did she care if O'Shea lived or died? She'd spent the last three years hating him and now she couldn't seem to stop thinking about him. So many unanswered questions still rolled around in her head. The crinkle of paper in her pocket reminded her that her mother had yet to speak. After everyone was patched up, Elisa intended on listening.

∞∞

Fortunately, Doctor Fredericks was a young man who'd recently replaced the aging Doctor Elijah. The new doctor had come from Houston and had lots of experience with surgery. He grimly mentioned that he'd been a surgeon during the war. An immediate bond was formed between Nate's Devils and the doc.

Elisa didn't let it bother her. As long as Dr. Fredericks did what he was supposed to do, that's all that mattered. She even pitched in fetching hot water and bandages. Elisa was surprised when Zeke assisted the doc. Apparently he'd been the medic for their cavalry unit during the war. He successfully patched up Nate and Jake while the doc focused on O'Shea. Jake had been first because he had a head wound, then he and Lee went to the saloon for a drink.

Elisa figured a shot of whiskey would taste mighty good, but she didn't even think of going yet. She stayed with Nate as he was doctored. The booze could wait, her nerves couldn't.

"What about your arm?" Nate asked as Zeke stitched up the wound on his fanny.

"It's a graze. I don't need any stitches." She pretended not to peek at the expanse of bare skin exposed when his britches were down.

"I don't care. You're going to let Zeke take a look." His black eyes bored into hers.

"Don't be bossy."

"Don't be stubborn."

"Can't help it."

"Neither can I."

Zeke cracked a smile. "You two are more entertaining than a show at the theater."

"Shut up, Zeke," Nate and Elisa chimed in together.

Zeke continued to smile as he put a bandage on the wound. "You were lucky, Nate. It went right through you, so I didn't have to dig anything out." He leveled his gaze at Elisa. "You're next."

She frowned. "You're as bossy as Gideon."

"I'll take that as a compliment." He finished Nate's bandage and went to the basin beside the examining table to wash his hands.

"It wasn't meant to be," Elisa grumbled.

"Now help your man with his trousers so you can get up here and let me look under your shirt."

Elisa snorted. "I didn't know you were funny."

"You don't know me at all." Zeke raised one blond eyebrow and Elisa laughed again.

"Stop flirting with my woman," Nate snapped.

"Don't get your knickers in a twist, Nate." Zeke slapped Nate's behind. "And get off the table."

"Ow!" Nate tried to smack Zeke, but he dodged out of the way.

"Boys." Elisa stood and helped Nate pull up his trousers enough so he could slide off the table and fasten them.

"Your turn." Nate grabbed her by the waist and plopped her on the table. "Do you want me to help you take your shirt off?"

Elisa glanced at Zeke who grinned broadly. "Both of you turn your backs."

With a dramatic groan, they turned around. Elisa slipped off her shirt, which was caked with dried blood, and wrapped a clean sheet around her, leaving the wounded arm exposed.

"You can turn around now."

Nate's gaze traveled up and down the exposed skin of her shoulders and arms. "You know how to tempt a man."

She shook her head. "Go check with the doc for me."

All teasing forgotten, he gave her a quick hug and a peck on the lips. "I'll be right back."

Zeke untied the makeshift bandage from her arm so gently, she almost didn't feel it. As he cleaned the wound, she bit her tongue to keep the moan of pain from escaping.

"Do you love him?"

She had expected the question, but not from Zeke. This smiling, flirting man was in complete contrast to the quiet, intense man she'd come to know. That put her on guard.

"None of your business."

"Listen, Elisa, everything to do with my friends is my business." The intense man was back and his brown eyes burned into hers like hot coals. "If you're looking for a man to warm your bed for a spell, then let him alone."

"I don't need a man," she scoffed. "Nate isn't warming my bed."

"Really?" Zeke's tone told her he knew different.

She fought the blush that threatened. "I mean, that's not what I want from him."

"Then what do you want?" He patted the wound dry.

"Everything."

Zeke studied her face for a full minute before nodding. "He's the man for that. Now are you going to answer the question?"

Elisa gritted her teeth as he dabbed some kind of paste on her. "I did."

"No you didn't, but you're very clever." He picked up a bandage from the table beside them. "Do you love him?"

"Yes, I do. Satisfied, you bully?" She hissed as he tightened the bandage.

"I'm not a bully and you know it. Nate is my brother as much as Lee is. I will never let anyone hurt him, including you." He handed her a clean shirt. "Doctor Fredericks left this for you."

"Thanks." She glanced down at her hands, still faintly stained by blood. "I won't hurt him."

Zeke nodded. "I believe you."

Nate poked his head in the door. "He's awake and asking for you, honey."

Elisa's heart jumped to her throat. "I'll be right there."

Zeke washed his hands, then gathered up the soiled linens and with a nod to both of them, left the room. Nate stepped in and walked over to her. She fought back the urge to throw her arms around him.

"You okay?" His brow was furrowed in concern.

"Yeah, I just need to gather my courage."

He saved her the trouble and wrapped his arms around her gently. She rested her head on his shoulder.

"After you talk to O'Shea, we need to talk." He kissed her temple. "Now get your shirt on and we'll go together."

She let the sheet fall, unembarrassed by her nudity, and pulled the shirt on with Nate's help. He buttoned her up, then pressed his lips to hers.

"Ready?" Nate asked.

"No, but let's go."

With Nate by her side, she headed toward her father, and the conversation that would steer the course for the rest of her life.

৪০০গ্ৰ

Lit only by a single kerosene lantern, the room sat in shadows. Elisa stepped in with Nate at her heels. O'Shea was tucked into a bed, as pale as the sheets surrounding him. His eyes opened and Elisa's step faltered.

"Come in here, girl. Leave him outside. Ain't none of his business."

She looked at Nate over her shoulder. He nodded and kissed her forehead.

"Call me if you need me." He shut the door behind him.

"Come closer. I ain't gonna bite." O'Shea's normally booming voice sounded so small.

Elisa stepped toward the bed and saw a stool placed right next to it. It took more courage to sit on that stool than it did to face down Rodrigo and his men. Her heart hammered as loud as a woodpecker in spring.

"You read those letters yet?"

She fingered them in her pocket. "No, haven't had a chance. Been busy."

He chuckled. "That you have. I hear tell you killed that bastard Rodrigo. I thank you for it. He about stole me blind."

"I didn't do it for you." She clenched her fists beneath the voluminous shirt.

"I know you didn't, but I'm grateful just the same." He sighed. "I thought you should know how you came to be and make peace with it."

"I'm listening." The last thing she wanted to be doing, but knew it had to be done.

"I met your mother when we was just kids. Fifteen or sixteen. Full of heat and love just like any young'uns. Ah, it was magic, girl, pure magic. We loved and before we knew it, she had caught pregnant." O'Shea blinked rapidly. "Her daddy was an important man in town, ya know. Had piles of money and knew how to throw it around. I was just a cow puncher who worked on the Grayton ranch, a nobody with no more than two bits to rub together. He used his money to get me put in prison for a year on some trumped-up charge."

"You were in prison?"

"I sent her piles of letters but never got any in return. By the time I was released, she'd married Sean Taggert and you were a wee babe. My heart near broke when I found out. I tried to see you, but old man Grayton threatened to put me in prison for life, or string me up from a cottonwood."

O'Shea finally looked her in the eye again. "You were a year old afore I got a look at you. Melissa was scared her daddy would do something so she told me to stay away. I made a vow to her that I'd get enough money to please her daddy so she could marry me. Only it never happened. I got the money all right, but she never left Taggert. Melissa wasn't strong enough to fight him. Her daddy died when you were eight and by then it was too late. She'd forgotten how much she loved me."

He reached out and touched her arm with a shaking hand. Elisa stared at the fingers, her rancor toward O'Shea fading.

"I gave you that horse. That was the first gift I could ever give you. I used to watch you ride it from that hill up near your house. You took to him like a duck to water." He smiled weakly. "You have your mother's beauty but you have my strength. Your mama, well she didn't want my money but she put it away for you. Everything I have is yours. I thought Sean had been killed in the war, I needed the stream for the cattle and I wanted to take care of both of you. I bought the land for more than it was worth, so you could be safe and have money to live." He shook his head. "Then when your ma died, I tried to help you, to take care of you, but dammit, girl, you fought me. When Sean came home, I didn't know what to do. I'd paid the two thousand and didn't get my land or my daughter. Sean was like a ghost, leaving you and your brother to work like dogs. I just wanted to help. Do you understand that, Elisa?"

Elisa had trouble swallowing the lump in her throat, but after she did, she was able to speak again. "I've hated you for three years. Lived, breathed and ate hate. I never knew...she used to stare out the window toward the north. I thought she just…I don't know what I thought. Now it all makes sense. It's going to take me some time to get over the hate."

Her mother had always been melancholy, never laughing and joking with the rest of them. A dark cloud seemed to hang over her head, as if joy had been sucked from her soul.

"I know. Read the letters. She wrote them while I was in prison, but never sent them to me. After her daddy died, she gave them to me. I…" He wiped his eyes with his left hand. "I loved her until she died. Never believed she killed herself."

The memory of finding her mother hanging from the roof rafter slammed into Elisa. She took two deep breaths and forced herself to focus on the here and now.

"From what Marchand tells me, Rodrigo killed her. One less person between him and my money." O'Shea sounded as bitter as she felt.

Anger surged fresh. "Damn, I wish I could kill him again."

O'Shea chuckled. "Ah, daughter, you and I, I think we'll get along just fine."

"Was he the one who tried to kidnap me too?" Elisa remembered that awful time when she hid in the woods for half a day from the men who'd tried to take her.

"I didn't know about that. Son of a bitch. I'm sorry that happened, Elisa." He reached out again and touched her.

Elisa glanced down at the hand on her arm. Slowly she turned her hand until it was palm up, then slid it under his. He closed his hand around hers.

It would take time, but she'd taken her first step toward the rest of her life.

80C3

Nate paced outside the room, straining to hear what they were saying. Their voices were too low, though, and he wished for the hundredth time that O'Shea had not thrown him out. He heard a commotion out in the front of the doctor's office, but ignored it. Elisa was more important.

When she stepped out of the room, he couldn't tell if she needed him or not. "Are you okay?"

"Yep. We've made our peace." She stepped past him and walked down the hallway.

"Wait, Elisa."

She turned and he saw a slight trembling in her chin. That was all he needed to know. As natural as rain falling in spring, she went into his arms and fit beneath his chin. He stroked her back without saying a word, giving her the time to compose herself.

"Will you marry me?" He had intended to make a romantic proposal, but sometimes his heart didn't listen to his brain.

She reared back and looked at him with narrowed eyes. "Is it because my real father is rich?"

It was Nate's turn to narrow his eyes. "I've been living with next to nothing all my life. Why would money be important now?"

"Are you sure?"

Nate knew he'd found where he was supposed to be and the woman he was supposed to love. "Yes, sweet Elisa, I'm sure."

"Okay then, I guess I'll marry you." She sounded as if she was agreeing to swallow castor oil.

Nate didn't care. He hooted and swung her around in a circle.

"Quit it, you're making me sick."

He set her back down and kissed her long and hard. When he finally released her lips, he grinned. "I love you, Elisa whatever-your-name-is."

She finally cracked a smile. "I love you too, Frenchie."

The commotion in the front of the office grew louder. Gideon was shouting. Nate grabbed Elisa's hand and ran toward the melee.

The scene that greeted them made Nate's entire body clench. Captain Nessman stood nose to nose with Gideon. Four blue coats were positioned near the door. Behind Gideon, Jake lay on a cot, his head swathed in bandages.

"You are not taking him, Captain. He has done nothing wrong and I refuse to allow you to take him into custody." Gideon rarely shouted, but now he was as loud as a brass band.

"Oh yes you will. Jacob Sheridan is my prisoner now. The judge granted me permission to bring him to Houston." The Yankee bastard held up a folded piece of paper.

"He was shot and beaten today. He's in no shape to go anywhere," the doctor interjected. "I don't care what that paper says."

God bless Doctor Fredericks.

"These men are here to assist me if you resist." Captain Nessman gestured at the soldiers, who looked entertained by the entire exchange.

"Captain Nessman," Nate said crisply as he stepped forward. "I'd like to see the judge's orders if I may."

Nessman held onto the paper as if his life depended on it. "You may not."

"Then you have no call to be here. If that's a paper issued by a judge in the state of Texas, then I have every right to look at it." Nate held out his hand, anger pulsing through him.

How dare the self-righteous son of a bitch continue to hound Jake over a fake charge of robbing a small general store? The entire thing was ridiculous.

Captain Nessman glared at the doctor. "You are to notify me when the prisoner is ready to be transported." He pointed at Gideon. "You will hand him over to me at that time."

"Like hell I will," Gideon snarled.

Nate stepped between them before blows were struck. The last thing they needed was Gideon in jail.

"Captain Nessman, the point of taking him into custody is moot. He's not fit to go anywhere but between the sheets until he heals." Nate gestured to the door. "He's not going to get better with all the shouting and hollering going on in here."

Nessman looked like he wanted to say something else, but he didn't. With a brisk nod to the doctor, he stomped out, followed by a blue trail of snickering privates.

"We need to get him out of here tonight." Gideon looked at his friends in turn. "I can't let that bastard take him."

"He won't. I promise you that." Zeke touched Jake's shoulder.

"I wasn't kidding when I said he couldn't be moved," Doctor Fredericks threw in. "You're going to have to wait at least one day before he can go anywhere."

"Then we leave tomorrow at dusk." Gideon glanced at Nate, then at Elisa, a question in his eyes.

Nate turned and held his hand out to Elisa. She stepped forward and planted her hand in his.

"I'm not sure I can leave with you. Elisa has agreed to marry me."

The words dropped like stones in a still pond. Expressions ranged from surprised, to pleased, to shocked.

Gideon nodded. "I had a feeling. You fixing on staying here with her and the boy?"

Nate looked down at Elisa, the woman who held his future in her hands. "There's a whole lot unsettled right now, and I can't leave her. But, I can't imagine being without the four of you."

His eyes stung with tears at the thought of not being with the Devils anymore. Not a morning had gone by in four years that they weren't together. It would be like losing his family.

"Well at least I won't have to listen to the creak from the starch in his drawers anymore," Lee drawled, a smirk on his face.

"And I won't have to listen to you complain," Nate countered.

Zeke, Lee and the doctor stepped forward to congratulate them. Gideon stayed where he was, staring at Nate. This would be the hardest part, saying goodbye to his best friend, his confidant, his brother.

He walked over to Gideon alone and held out his hand. Gideon glanced at his hand and pulled Nate into a hug instead.

"We'll be back as soon as we can shake Nessman." Gideon cleared his throat and wiped his right eye with his thumb. "I'm glad you found her. She's, ah, just what you needed."

"Thanks, Gid. I'll be working on the legal side of getting Jake's name cleared from here. I know O'Shea will help." Nate's throat was coated with unshed tears that fell down into his soul. "I'll miss you."

Gideon's blue gaze grew suspiciously moist. "I'll miss you too."

They hugged again.

"Well, geez, Elisa, you may have to pry them apart with a stick," Jake's raspy voice interrupted.

Everyone laughed and Nate knew all would be well with his friends. He'd make a life with Elisa and keep his friends in his heart.

೮೦೧೪

The next day, the Devils were packed to leave before the sun set. Nate bade them all goodbye and hugged each of them, even Lee, who made the grand gesture of hugging him back. O'Shea had given them five hundred dollars. It was enough to keep the four of them alive for a while.

Elisa stood behind them quietly, lending her support by simply being there. She could see Nate struggling to say goodbye. Her heart pinched for him, but it also rejoiced because she had a man who loved her, who was willing to do what he needed to stay with her.

The redhead Jake appeared at her side, his freckles standing out on the pale skin. "He's a good man." Although he was still swathed in bandages, he was ready to leave with his friends.

Elisa nodded. "I think so too."

"Please don't hurt him. Nate has always been a good friend and a better brother." Jake's blue eyes were serious, a condition she suspected didn't happen often.

"I promise, I'll never hurt him. At least on purpose."

Jake pulled her into a quick hug. "Nate's a lucky man."

Elisa couldn't contain her surprise. "You're the charmer, aren't you?"

"Guilty." He winked. "And no more shooting at him, okay? We'd like him in one piece."

"I swear, no more shooting at him." She laughed, a bright spot in a day of ghosts and shadows.

Jake kissed her cheek then joined his friends, the hat hiding the bandage on his forehead. Just like that the four of them disappeared into the fading light of dusk.

ഇയങ്ങ

Nate's heart felt heavy as he watched them ride away. He turned to find Elisa on the sidewalk, waiting patiently. He put his arms around her, pulling her close and breathing in her scent.

"I'm going to miss them."

"They'll miss you too." She lightly scratched at his back. "I suspect they'll be back sooner than you think."

"Let's go home." Nate pulled back and stared into her eyes. "Unless you want to stop at the preacher's house and get hitched."

Elisa's eyes widened. "Today?"

"Why not, you have something else to do?" The more he thought about it, the better the idea sounded. "Today is a day of new beginnings. Let's start again. Together."

She raised one eyebrow. "Does that mean we get a wedding night?"

Nate laughed and swung her around in a circle. "Every night for the rest of our lives."

As he held her close, Nate realized that he might have stumbled upon Grayton a poor, desperate man. Now he had riches beyond his wildest imaginings and a woman who lived in his heart.

Life began again in a tiny town in Texas for the first Devil from Georgia.

About the Author

You can't say cowboys without thinking of Beth Williamson. She likes 'em hard, tall and packing. Read her work and discover for yourself how hot and dangerous a cowboy can be.

Beth lives in North Carolina, with her husband and two sons. Born and raised in New York, she holds a B.F.A. in writing from New York University. She spends her days as a technical writer, and her nights immersed in writing hot romances for her readers.

To learn more about Beth Williamson, please visit http://www.bethwilliamson.com/. Send an email to Beth at beth@bethwilliamson.com, join her Yahoo! Group, http://groups.yahoo.com/group/cowboylovers, or sign up for Beth's monthly newsletter, Sexy Spurs on her website.

Look for these titles

Can a man who lives in the shadows and a woman who lives in the light find a place to belong together?

The Tribute
© *2007 Beth Williamson*

Brett Malloy has always been considered a loner, a man apart from the Malloy clan. Quiet, reserved and intense, Brett hides from the world on his new ranch with only an ex-gunslinger and a runaway boy for company. When circumstances put him flat on his back, his childhood crush, Doctor Alexandra Brighton arrives to nurse him back to health.

Alex has always loved Brett despite the fact that a more difficult man couldn't be found on the face of the earth. A woman who firmly believes everyone should live life to the fullest, Alex takes Brett's quiet surliness as a mission. She's going to teach him what it means to live, and how to find love and passion in the most unexpected places.

When rancher King Dawson claims Alex as his own, Brett has to choose between the darkness of his shadows and the light of Alex's love.

Available now in ebook from Samhain Publishing.

hot
stuff

Discover Samhain!
THE HOTTEST NEW PUBLISHER ON THE PLANET

Romance, fantasy, mystery, thriller, mainstream and
more—Samhain has more selection, hotter authors, and
everything's available in both ebook and print.

Pick your favorite, sit back, and enjoy the ride!
Hot stuff indeed.

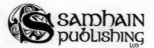